ALAN GARNER was born in Congleton, Cheshire in 1934, and grew up in Alderley Edge, where his father's family had lived for more than three hundred years. He was educated at Manchester Grammar School and at Magdalen College, Oxford, after which he began writing his first novel, *The Weirdstone of Brisingamen*, at the age of twenty-two. His books include *Elidor*, *The Owl Service* (which won the *Guardian* Award and the Carnegie Medal), *Red Shift* and *The Stone Book Quartet*, recognised by the Phoenix Award of America for 1996.

Alan Garner

STRANDLOPER

THE HARVILL PRESS
LONDON

for Patsy
and
for Narig:n

First published in in 1996
by The Harvill Press, 84 Thornhill Road, London N1 1RD

This paperback edition first published in 1997

18

Copyright © Alan Garner, 1996

Glyphs drawn from nineteenth-century sources, by Griselda Greaves

A CIP catalogue record for this book is available from the British Library

ISBN 9781860461613

Designed and typeset in Joanna at the Libanus Press, Marlborough

Half title photograph by Robert Mort

Penguin Random House is committed to a sustainable future for our business, our readers and our planet. This book is made from Forest Stewardship Council® certified paper.

MIX
Paper from
responsible sources
FSC® C018179

Printed and bound in Great Britain by Clays Ltd, Elcograf S.p.A.

I

SHICK-SHACK

"Fare Forth," said the Three Men, "and keep your promise.
By the bole of this broad tree We bide you here"

II

CRANK CUFFIN

And there he makes fast his feet and gropes about,
and stands up in that stomach that stank as the devil.
There in grease and filth that flavoured of hell
He built his stall, that would no harm take.

III

YOUNG COB

Over many cliffs he climbs in countries strange,
For parted from his friends, as a stranger he rides.

IV

MURRANGURK

From that spot my spirit there sprang in space.
My body on grave mound lay. In dreaming
My ghost is gone in His grace
On quest that moves in Mystery.

V

STRANDLOPER

We all go to the bones
all of them shining white in this Dulur country,
The noise of our father Bunjil
rushing down singing in this heart of mine.

NOTE

Much of what follows did happen; but I have been free with historical detail, in order to make clear the pattern.

A. G.

I

SHICK-SHACK

"Fare forthe," quoþ þe Frekez, "and fech as þou seggez;
By bole of þis brode tre We byde þe here"

"Cleanness"
lines 621/22

I

I sing the eagle.

"Bone of the Cloud. The Clashing Rock. The Hard Darkness."

It hangs above the grave mound.

I sing, dreaming.

"Tharangalkbek."

He sings the eagle into him.

"In the Beginning, when the waters parted and the Ancestors Dreamed all that is, and woke the life that slept, the sky lay on the earth, and the sun could not move, until the Magpie lifted the sky with a stick."

Nullamboin sings.

The women danced.

> "Kiminary keemo,
> Kiminary keemo,
> Kiminary kiltikary, kiminary keemo.
> String stram pammadilly, lamma pamma rat tag,
> Ring dong bomminanny keemo."

They danced around Tiddy Turnock's hollow oak: Martha Slater, Ann Shaw, Sarah Baguley, Phoebe Foden, Matty Rathbone, Betty Barns. The oak was too wide for them to join hands; split in four, it was big enough to keep a bull in. And the oak danced, curving its four backs, flinging their heads out to the wind.

> "Kiminary keemo,
> Kiminary keemo,
> Kiminary kiltikary, kiminary keemo.
> String stram pammadilly, lamma pamma rat tag,
> Ring dong bomminanny keemo."

The inside of the oak was filled with young men: Elijah Edge, Charlie Massey, Isaac Slater, Sam Thorley, John Stayley, Niggy Bower, William Buckley and Joshua Slack. They were playing hoodman blind, and Esther Cumberbach had a rolled up ground net of yellow silk about her eyes. Near the tree, by his horse, Edward Stanley wrote in a pocket book. William Buckley's lurcher lay on the ground, its head on its paws, watching the game.

The women started to clap their hands, and the pace of the dance increased.

> "Kiminary keemo,
> Kiminary keemo,
> Kiminary kiltikary, kiminary keemo.
> String stram pammadilly, lamma pamma rat tag,
> Ring dong bomminanny keemo."

The dog pricked its ears. It lifted its head, and looked about, sniffed, as though hearing, searching for, something.

Then, its belly and tail low, it slunk for Esther Cumberbach and took hold of the hem of her skirt and began to tug at it, growling, not fiercely, its teeth bared and eyes rolling. Esther squealed in laughter.

"Gerroff, Gyp!"

But the dog did not let go. It jerked backwards, tripping the men.

"Gyp! Gerroff!"

William Buckley waved at the dog, but he dared not make any sound, and the dog ignored him. The game was now rampage, and the women laughed and screamed in excitement, as the men staggered and Esther struggled for her balance, lost it and was pulled off her feet. Her outstretched arms clutched William about his waist. The dog let go of her skirt and stood, wagging its tail and panting. Esther undid the net from her eyes.

"It's you, Will."

"Oh heck." But he grinned.

Esther opened the net and cast it over William. The others all shouted, and the men caught hold of him and spun him around in the net until he was entangled and giddy. They chanted:

> "Shick-Shack, penny a rag!
> Bang his head in Cromwell's bag!
> All up in a bundle!"

The men lifted him and ran with him out of the tree, down the field and across the lane to the mere. They held him by his arms and legs and swung him to the rhythm of their chant. The women joined in:

> "Shick. Shack. Shick.
> Shick. Shack. Shick.
> Brick-y Buck-ley,
> You . . . Are . . . It . . . "

And they flung the great size of him as far as they could over the water. Edward Stanley stood apart, writing in his book.

William floundered in the net, trying to get to his feet. His head appeared above the water.

"Buggers!"

He rose out of the mere. He was only up to his knees, but the mud and leaves blackened and clung to him. He hopped to the bank, falling, coughing, spouting water, laughing, and the others scattered before him, up and down, as he wriggled to free himself. Esther and Edward watched.

"Shick-Shack!"

They were too nimble. He blundered around, and they ran under his arms, and his feet slipped on the grass. He fell, and lay there, breathless, spitting. Esther and the dog sat by him. She picked the net clean, crushed it and put it in her bodice.

"Good lad, Bricky!" shouted Sam Thorley.

"Penny a rag!"

"Buggers." He wiped his mouth, and laughed.

"You're gratified, aren't you?" said Edward.

"Eh?"

"You're glad."

"Oh ay."

"Him," said Esther; "he's pleased as Punch."

"Be good, William!"

"Be good, Sarah!"

They were leaving; the job done. He waved to them.

"Let's be having you," she said. "Off home and under the pump."

"It's muck and water," he said. "It'll dry. Eh! How about that? Shick-Shack."

"You'll catch your death," she said.

"I'll take no harm."

"You will for reading," said Edward.

He dabbled his fingers in the water, and wiped them on grass. "Will they do?"

"They'll do," said Edward, and turned and led the way back from the mere to the oak. William, the dog and Esther followed. It was coming on to rain: a shower; and at the back of it a bright sun.

When they were inside the tree, they sat down, and Edward took a book and some folded sheets of paper from his coat pocket. He gave the paper to William. "Here's your hand practice," he said. "You've got the pen and ink at home?"

William nodded.

"Then copy it tonight, and have it ready for me after Morning Service."

"I'll do me best, Yedart."

"And this," said Edward. He gave William the book.

"Eh! Isn't it your father's?"

The arms of Stanley were emblazoned on the leather: an eagle preying on a swaddled infant.

"He doesn't read."

"I'll be summonsed."

"Hanged, more like," said Esther.

"He'll not miss it," said Edward. "But see you keep it clean."

"Oh, I shall."

He held the book as if it were a bird.

"Can I have a go?"

"Yes."

"Now?"

"Of course you may."

"Where must I start?"

"Here. Where the poem begins."

"Poem? I can't read poem, me."

"You haven't tried," said Edward.

[7]

Esther reached into a cranny in the oak root and lifted out the shiny pebbles she kept there.

"Play jackstones," she said.

"We're reading," said William.

"I'll play meself, then," she said, and tossed and caught the pebbles. They chinked together, like glass.

William stared at the page.

"Try," said Edward.

He strove to lift the words with his eyes, to drag the sound from his tongue, against the ringing of the jackstones.

> "'Of Mans First Disobedience, and the Fruit
> Of that Forbidden Tree – '"

He was sweating. Esther snatched at the shiny pebbles.

"' – whose mortal tast Brought Death into the World, and all our woe, With loss of Eden'. Het, give over. I can't think."

Esther sniffed, and went on at the jackstones.

"Yet leave it for now," said Edward. "I'll hear you tomorrow. Look after that book, or my father will have the hide off me." He wrapped it in a handkerchief. "There. Read that when you're dry."

William put the writing paper with the book, and stuck the bundle inside his shirt. Esther dropped the jackstones into the root. Edward mounted his horse.

"Real writing, Yedart?"

"Real writing, Will. The best you are able."

He rode away. William and Esther settled back in the dead leaves of last year. "Are you not cold?" she said.

"Never."

The tree enclosed them.

She picked the twigs and rubbish from the mere off his chest, teasing.

> "'Oh, can you wash a soldier's shirt?
> And can you wash it clean?

Oh, can you wash a soldier's shirt,
                And hang it on the green?' "
"And whatever's that?"
"What me father and them sing when they're coming home from Bull's Head."
"How's it go?"
" 'Oh, can you wash a soldier's shirt?' " said Esther. " 'And can you wash it clean?' "
" 'Oh, can you wash a soldier's shirt – '?"
" 'And hang it on the green?' "
"It's good, that," said William.

He looked up through the empty crown. Above it a kestrel fluttered, its wings blurred, its tail curved. He pursed his lips and made clicking sounds.

"What's to do?" said Esther.
"Cush, cush; cush-a-cush."
"What is it?"
"A windhover. Cush-a-cush."
"It's nobbut a brid," said Esther.
The kestrel swerved out of sight.

William stood up, and pulled Esther to her feet, and they left the oak. He took her by the hand, and they walked down to the mere, the dog close behind.

The shower was passing: a drizzle so fine that the drops hung in the sun.

"See at the rainbow!"

An alder grew from the bank, its trunk lying on the mere, and the rainbow plunged into the branches of its head, snared in a willow.

"I've never been so near," said Esther. She was whispering. "See at it."
"Eh up. Cush-a-cush."

The kestrel was above the rainbow. It shut its wings and stooped into the alder, but they did not see it rise again. It was lost in the dazzle of colour.

"I've never been so near," said Esther. She went along the willow.

"It'll shift," said William. "It will. As good as goose skins." But he went to her, by the alder. The dog tested each step of the trunk. They sat in the branches. "I told you." The rainbow was out on the water.

"But it was here," said Esther. "Here's where it was." They held each other.

"Eh, but Shick-Shack. Me."

"What's all this reading for?" she said.

"It's Yedart."

"I know that."

"He's learning me."

"But what's it for?"

"It betters you."

"How?"

He shrugged. "Yedart says."

" 'Yedart says'! Ay. And Yedart does. You've been all nowtiness and discontent since you started this caper."

"I like it."

"But what does it mean? What you were reading back there."

"Anyone can do it."

"Well, I can't."

"Yay, but you can."

He caught hold of her wrist, and wrote with her hand in the water. I. Do. Love. Thee.

She pulled her hand clear. The water shimmered, and was still.

"I do love thee," he said.

"And I do love thee," she said. "But you'll get that slutch off first. I'm not sitting up with any crow-trod gowf tonight."

He tried to kiss her. "No. Not while you get that slutch off."

"I do love you, Het."

She laughed, and splashed water at him. She reached down to scoop more, but her fingers caught on a hardness in the mud. She took it, and put it into his hand.

"There. Don't say I never give you nothing."

It was a stone; a black stone; flecked with red; part bubbled as a brain, part rough as frost; and all stuck about with clear crystals that winked in the light.

He held it on his palm.

"It's a swaddledidaff," she said.

"From the end of the rainbow."

"Our swaddledidaff. From me to thee."

The rainbow was gone.

2

"Shick-Shack, eh?" said Grandad.

"Ay." said William.

They were at the table in the farm kitchen. Esther stood at a side-board, eating the same food: hot water, flour and bacon grease over boiled potatoes on a tin plate, with a lump of fat bacon. They drank buttermilk from mugs.

Grandad laughed. "Dear, dear! Eh, dear!" He spooned potato into his mouth, holding the bacon in the other hand, nibbling the meat. "And who's Teaser?"

"She is."

"She's never!"

"I am, that!" said Esther.

Both men laughed.

"Fecks!" said Grandad. "It's got the makings of a rollicking good year! The two on you?"

They ate.

"Fecks!" Grandad spluttered into his potatoes and grease. They all laughed.

"Side the table, Het," said William.

The meal was over, and he went to a corner cupboard that hung on the wall and took out a quill and ink-horn and the paper that Edward Stanley had given him. Esther cleared the table, and Grandad sat in the man's chair by the fire. William laid out the materials with care, while Esther scraped the plates in a pancheon of cold water.

"Did you find me a dish or owt while you were at Congleton, Mr Buckley?" said Esther.

"Oh, ay. I was forgetting," said Grandad, "what with all the to do;" and he leant down and rummaged in a sack that was on the floor. "There was this here in the market. Ever such a nice gentleman, called Mr Minton, from Spode, out of Pottery, he had a stall, and I fancied this."

"Eh! It's grand!" said Esther. She wiped her hands on her skirt, and took the plate that Grandad was holding and carried it to the window. "How much shall you be stopping out of me wages?"

"Not much," said Grandad. "Say half a day. You see, I had three pullets with me; and this Mr Minton, a very clever gentleman he must be to have made yon, he took to them pullets, so it was 'swoppery no robbery'. He was that pleased, I didn't like to tell him as two on them had gone light and were off their legs."

"See at this, Will," said Esther.

"What is it?" William had been only half listening as he gathered himself to write.

"China."

"What's china?"

"This is."

"And what good's that?"

"It's for looking. See at it!"

The plate was round and white, edged with a pattern. In the middle was a landscape: a fence, and beyond it three buildings, and a boat and boatman on a river and a bridge across. Three figures were on the bridge. There were two big trees, one a willow, and, in the sky, two birds flying. And both edging and picture were in blue.

"And that's china?" said William.

"Ay."

"But what's china? Is it pot or is it picture?"

"I don't know," said Esther.

"Rum place, if it is," said William. "I've never known folks be blue." And he sat down at the table to write.

Esther put the plate on the sideboard. "It's grand," she said. "Thanks ever so much, Mr Buckley."

"Ay, well, just so long as you're pleased," said Grandad.

"Oh, I am," said Esther, and she gave the plate one more look before she went back to scraping the tin.

Grandad lit his pipe and stared into the fire.

"Best year were when Shick-Shack were Squarker Kennerley," said Grandad, "and Three-quarter Sarah, she were Teaser. By! I recollect there was some Christenings March following. Bigod, ay! What? There was some Christenings!"

William looked at the writing exercises, and read each one before copying it. The ink had run in the wet of his shirt. His lips moved. Then he wrote, holding the quill upright, and steering it with his little finger.

"But Squarker were a bugger for cross-cutting when I were top man at the pit, and he were bottom. You can be cross-cutting a piece of timber, two on you as know what cross-cutting is, and it isn't hard work; but get one as doesn't know what it is, and he'll maul your belly out; and yet he thinks he's working! He is! And hard work for you and all! 'I don't mind you having a ride, but keep your feet up!' That's what I tell 'em. And they look at me like a cow at a cabbage."

William read what he had copied.

" 'The strongest poison ever known
Came from Caesar's laurel crown.' "

He started the next exercise.

"Ay," said Grandad. "But, oh, they'll murder you, some of them will, for cross-cutting. Oh no, bigod, they're murderous! But they don't know they're doing it. Squarker didn't. Oh, ay! He had to go."

William read: " 'A rumour is spread from the south, and it is terrible to tyrants'."

"I recollect, when Waggy Worth was wheelwright," said Grandad.

"Eh up. We're off," said Esther. " 'Waggy's Coffin'."

"Ay," said Grandad. "This chap had died, like, and Waggy'd nowt put him in, sort of thing; and he come to the pit for us to cut him a suit of coffin stuff. And it was that clean, the wood, you know, he'd stop a bit extra long and have another suit cut, you see."

Esther finished her tidying and sat by the fire, but she did not settle. William read: " 'Ancient abuses are not by their antiquity converted into virtues'."

"And then Tiddy Turnock," said Grandad, "he was there, and he said, 'Ay,' he said, 'it'd pay a man for to die to have a suit of this sort!' And that were it. Ay! Waggy had it in the week, right enough. He picked his mortal own coffin. 'Well,' he said, 'I'll have that, and I'll have that, and I'll have that. And a bit of old shelving will do for the bottom.' And he had it hisself in the week, bigod. Ay!"

" 'Man has rights which no statutes or usages take away'."

"Have you not done, yet?" said Esther.

"Wait on," said William.

"Hold still," said Grandad. "You're up and down like a dog at a fair."

"It was in the hiring," said Esther. "It's what were agreed. Saturday night's for sitting up."

" 'And lasses is lads' leavings.' "

"Hush up, Grandad," said William. " 'They little think how dangerous it is to let the people know their power.' "

"And you think on, and all," said Grandad. " 'A slice off a cut loaf isn't missed,' is it? It's there, you know. Oh yes! A slice off a cut loaf isn't missed."

William laughed, and put the writing in the cupboard, and took out the book. He looked at the eagle and child. Grandad leaned

forward in his chair, and pointed with his forefinger, waving his
hand away from him.

"What's that article?" he said.

"A book," said William.

"And whose book?" The hand was in a palsy.

"Stanleys'."

"Sarn it! My stockings, youth! If yon's found here, you'll piss before
you'll whistle!"

"I tell't him," said Esther.

"I've only lent it; from Yedart. He's a chap very fluent in giving."

The hand stopped its shaking, and the finger jabbed at the leather.

"Yay?" said Grandad. "Giving? With that lot, it runs in th' blood like
wooden legs!"

"Haven't you done?" said Esther.

"Not yet," said William.

"Oh, what the heck," said Esther.

Grandad sat back in his chair and stared into the fire. He muttered
to himself. William opened the book, studied it for a while, and
began to read aloud. Esther poked the fire, rattling the irons against
his voice.

> " 'I thence
> Invoke thy aid to my adventrous Song,
> That with no middle flight intends to soar
> Above th' Aonian Mount'

—What's th' Aonian Mount? Is it a horse or summat?"

"I shouldn't wonder," said Grandad.

> " — 'Above th' Aonian Mount, while it pursues
> Things unattempted yet in Prose or Rime.' "

Esther flung the irons down and shouted, "Will Buckley! Are you
coming, or aren't you?"

William grinned, and closed the book. He looked at the

emblazoning again.

"You'll do, Het. You'll do."

He put the book with the writing in the cupboard and shut it. He took Esther by the hand.

"Here, Gyp."

The dog rose from the fire and came to heel.

"Good night, Grandad."

"Good night, Mr Buckley," said Esther.

"Eh!" said Grandad. "And when you're in that barn, watch your twiddle-diddles. There's rats."

William, Esther and the dog left the kitchen. Grandfather stared back at the fire. "No. A slice off a cut loaf isn't missed – unless you cut too deep."

3

"Boneless!!"

He sat up, flailing his head and arms. The dog yelped and leapt to the wall, barking.

"Shurrup, Gyp!" Esther shouted. The dog whined.

"Boneless!"

"Wake up, love. You're dreaming."

"Boneless. It's Boneless!"

She held him, and he stank of fear.

"It was a bad dream," she said; but, awake now, there was terror still in him, and he shook and nestled into her, a child, sobbing.

"It's him. It's Boneless."

"You make no sense."

The sobbing died, and the only sound was his breath, deep and quick. She held him.

"What's 'Boneless'?" said Esther.

The words fell from him, without pause, broken only by the rasping air.

"It's Boneless come for to ketch me, and Granny calls me a nowt and tells me get back to sleep, but I can't, I'm that feart.

"Then me Grandad, he sends me go robmawkin on Tiddy Turnock. And Tiddy has this mawkin in his field, and it isn't any old mawkin. No. Tiddy must have summat different; and he's rigged up this contraption, like a gallows, sort of thing, with the mawkin hanging from it, and clog soles on its arms for clattering, and the whole lot turns in the wind. Well, me Grandad fancies the red weskit and the britches that are on this here mawkin; so he gives me his own weskit and britches and sends me for fetch Tiddy's. So I go. I'm only little. And this mawkin is big. Tiddy's made it out of old sacks and stuffed them with grass, and cut holes for the face, and the grass is sticking out of its eyes and its nose and out of its mouth, and I don't like it, not one bit.

"Anyroad, I ketches hold on it, and I'm carrying Grandad's weskit and britches, and I tries get weskit and britches off mawkin, but it won't hang still. It keeps twisting and turning, and seems like it's ketching hold on me instead. And then it falls over, on top of me, and its great face and all that grass are staring at me in the moon, and it's soft and then it's Boneless; and I let out such a skrike, and run all the way back home. And doesn't Grandad tan my hide! But ever since, that mawkin comes at me, and I know it's Boneless."

"There, love," said Esther. "It's gone now. It was a dream."

"It's real," said William. "But it's different tonight. I know him. And sky's purple."

"Who is he, then?" said Esther.

"I'm his uncle. But I can't be, can I? And he wants summat. He wants me to get him summat."

"What?"

"A crow. He wants me get him a crow. That's daft. Mawkins are for scaring crows, not fetching them."

"Eh, dear. Best be doing, love," said Esther. "It's light already, see." The day was shining through the cracks in the wall panels of the barn, between the timbers.

"And I've got a sick headache," said William.

"Where's it hurt?"

"Here. This side. I'm bilious."

"You're always the same, you, after sitting up."

[19]

"I can't help it. I'm bilious."

"Come here," said Esther. "Give us your head."

William lifted his head out of her lap, and she cradled it, stroking his brow. She sang.

> " 'Lu lay, lu lay,
> Lu lara lay;
> Bayu, bayu,
> Lu lara lay;
> Hush-a-bye, lu lay.' "

"Sing that again."

> " 'Lu lay, lu lay,
> Lu lara lay;
> Bayu, bayu,
> Lu lara lay;
> Hush-a-bye, lu lay.' "

"I like that."

There was the clumping of boots outside the barn, and a stick banged on the walls.

"Come on! Let's be having you! Cow wants milking! And you! Get the straw out of your arse and lay the fire!"

"He's got a sick headache!" said Esther, trying to be loud without hurting.

"What the ferrips do you get up to, the pair on you?" shouted Grandad. "You must be a right un!"

"He's bilious!"

"Bilious be buggered! I want my breakfast!"

Esther pulled her clothes together. "You stay there," she whispered. "I'll see to the old devil." She went out of the barn, opening the door as little as she could, to keep the dark. "I'm coming! Wait your sweat!"

William lay in the straw, his hands to his head, moaning. The dog snarled. He opened his eyes.

"No."

The timbers of the barn, wall and roof glowed and shimmered with rainbow patterns: lines, curved and crooked; dots, spots and twisted circles; some like the shapes he saw in his head when the pain was bad, but not all; and every one was on the timber, and on only the timber, leaving no space. The wood was carved with light. And the May dawn wind that was blowing around the barn carried a sound in it, like none he had ever heard, unless it was women wailing; but never as he had heard women; and it was faint, though near. And the dog heard it, he could see, and the dog was watching the light in the wood, too.

"Bloody no."

He threw the door open and ran into the sun, which screamed in his brain, but this he knew, and he ran to the house and into the kitchen and threw himself onto the settle. The dog stayed in the barn, watching.

"Lie still," said Esther; and she left the fire and poured vinegar into a bowl, steeped a cloth in the vinegar, squeezed it, and laid it as a poultice on William's forehead.

"I'm badly. I'm badly."

"Lie still," she said again. "It's best."

And he lay still, all through the morning, his eyes shut, because of the light that was sound; and the sound that was lights slowly changed back to the right way, and the pain died, until he heard a thrush and a blackbird singing, clear as dew, the only sounds in the world, as they were when the sick headache left him.

Esther came and sat with him. She washed the china plate, and dried it with a clean cloth. "It's beautiful," she said. "Isn't it? I wonder who all them folks are: him in the boat, and three on the bridge. And what are they doing? Fishing, or running or what? And

[21]

they've all getten pigtails. Are they sailors?" But he was too weak to move, and he fell into a sleep.

The dog's barking woke him. A horse stopped in the lane, and there was a knock at the door. Esther went to open it, and he heard her talking.

"Who is it?" shouted Grandad from beside the fire. "What they wanting?"

"It's Mr Yedart."

"Let him in!"

Grandad pushed Esther aside. He spoke a formal welcome, broadening his voice to the custom.

"Come thi ways within air o' th' fire, Mr Yedart, and get some warmship."

Edward Stanley took off his hat and entered.

"Good day to you, Mr Buckley, sir."

"Sit thi down. Tek thi bacca. Stick thi nose up chimney," said Grandad, ending the ritual.

Edward smiled his thanks, but refused the man's chair, taking one from beside the table. "And when and at what hour is the churching?" he said.

"That's for you to ask and us to know," said Grandad.

"Ah. Then what is wrong with you, William?" said Edward.

"It's an allegar poultice for his sick headache," said Esther.

" 'Sick headache'!" said Grandad. "Yay. And you ask him how he gets them Saturday nights regular! 'Sick headache', ay, bigod. He's a right un. Soft as me pocket. 'Sick headache'! So what's he going to do with cockle-bread? 'Sick headache', as sure as a red pig for an acorn!"

William started to pull himself up, but Edward stopped him. "Stay there," he said. "I've come for your hand practice, and to leave you some other."

"Will Sir John not be vexed?" said Grandad.

"How shall he be vexed when he does not know?" said Edward.

"He doesn't mind his servants reading," said Esther.

"I'm no servant," said Grandad, "and I don't read."

Edward laughed. "He suffers reading because servants may take instruction thereby. But with writing: with writing, one may instruct. There he is not so generous. And noise of revolution aids little."

"Ay, well, here's what youth wrote last night," said Grandad, and opened the cupboard and gave Edward the sheets of paper and the emblazoned book. "And I'd be a sight happier if yon were out of this house. I'm not inclined to dance at the sheriff's ball, me."

"It would never come to that," said Edward. "You have my word."

"Yay," said Grandad.

Edward looked at the sheets. His face stiffened. He looked again, closely.

"William. What is this?" His voice was cold.

"Real writing, Yedart."

"'Real writing'? This?"

"The best I was able," said William.

"This?"

Edward pulled the cloth from William's brow and thrust the paper at him. William looked, through half-closed eyes, which opened when he saw. There were no exercises. Below each example were drawn patterns of dots and circles and waves and zigzag and criss-crossed lines, many as he had seen in the barn, some as on the blue plate; and the last example had under it the shape of a serpent made up of the parts in the foolish lines.

"I never!"

"I do not risk my father's wrath," said Edward, "in order to be made a mockery by a peasant."

"I never."

"You shall fulfil your promise, as I have seen it in you. You will

[23]

write this again."

Edward flung more paper onto the settle and stalked to the door. "Your servant, Mr Buckley," he said, and he pointed the word.

"Leave the book!" William shouted. "Don't take me brid and babby!"

" 'Brid and babby'?" said Edward. He opened the book, and read aloud. " 'What in me is dark illumine, what is low raise and support; that to the heighth of this great Argument I may assert Eternal Providence, and justify the ways of God to men.' " It would seem that you may have work to do yet, William, before you are competent to philosophise on matters such as this." And he snapped the book shut, thrust it into his pocket and left the room. Esther closed the door after him.

William stared at the paper and at what had been done.

"Well, you've flewen high and let in a cow clap at last," said Grandad. "And no error."

William swung his feet down to the floor. "I wrote proper. I did."

" 'But when, quoth Kettle to his mare,' " said Grandad.

William took out the pen and ink and sat at the table. He spread the paper and began to write.

"I'll show him. I did."

"Anyroad, it looks like you've forgotten your sick headache," said Grandad.

4

Grandad and William walked up the lane to the church. The dog followed.

"You've not a great lot to say for yourself."

"I'm feart," said William. "I might cack me."

"Feart of what?" said Grandad.

"All them words; if I can't remember."

"Eh, youth! You've heard them every mortal Shick-Shack Day since you were that high! You'll not forget."

"But standing up in front, and the vicar and that."

"Oh, give over."

"And no one ever sees churching. What must I do?"

"I'll be with you. You'll be right. But if you're not one for it, you must say. Else, it'll be too late."

"For what?"

"What you didn't ought."

"But what happens?"

"You'll be asked three times. And if you can't answer, that's it."

"Have you been Shick-Shack?"

"My stars and garters and little apples!" said Grandad. "Yon blob-tongue won't be told, will he?"

Edward Stanley was sitting by his tethered horse at the church gate. He stood as they approached. Grandad blocked the gate with his body.

"I've come for the churching," said Edward.

"It's not for you, nor the likes of you," said Grandad. "Leave churching to us."

"God's House is for all men," said Edward.

"Not today, it isn't. Now you bugger off out."

"You shall not deny me," said Edward.

"Shall I not?"

The dog growled, and paced towards Edward, stiff-legged, its ears flat, and front lip raised, pushing back its nose.

Edward lifted his riding crop.

"I don't recommend as you try that," said Grandad. "He's not one for being hit."

The dog paced each step slowly, but without hesitating. Edward moved back.

"I recollect he has a flavour for red meat," said Grandad.

Edward untethered the horse and mounted awkwardly. It was restless, and turned from the dog.

"Go be cock on your own midden," said Grandad.

The horse moved sideways into the road. Edward held a short rein as its hooves scraped.

" 'Home to thi daddy, my little laddy,' " said Grandad. The horse carried Edward away. "Beggaring allsorts. Buggering whopstraws. They'd own body and soul, if you let 'em, and still they'd know nowt."

Grandad and William went through the gateway and up the mound to the church. The church was a frame of timber, with a belfry and chancel; the south porch an arch of curved trunks carved. Grandad stopped at the arch and set William before him. Only then did William see that the wardens were standing on either side of the door, their dark dress blending with the dark oak, the brass of their staffs glinting in the depth of the porch.

"Gripe, griffin, hold fast," said Squarker Kennerley. And Grandad took hold of William by his upper arms.

"Jack Miller asketh help to turn his mill aright," said Tiddy Turnock. "He hath grounden small, small."

"The King's Son of Heaven," said Squarker, "He shall pay for all."

"With right and with might," they both shouted, "with skill and with will; let might help right, and skill go before will, and right before might, so goeth our mill."

"Gripe, griffin, hold fast," said Grandad.

"Falseness and guile," said Tiddy, "have reigned too long."

"And truth," said Squarker, "hath been set under a lock."

"And falseness and guile," said Tiddy, "reigneth in every stock."

"True love is away," said Squarker, "that was so good."

"And clerks for wealth," said Tiddy, "work them woe."

"God do bote!" they shouted. "For now is time!"

The wardens opened the church door.

"Shick-Shack," said Squarker, "enter in."

"And when you enter on a thing," said Tiddy, "think you, too, on its ending."

"Gripe, griffin, hold fast," said Grandad, and pushed William forward into the church, firming his arms tight.

The wardens closed the door, and led the way into the hall and forest of the church sunrising around the font and back to a window by the door. The church was quiet, except for a bee that had woken late in the warmth and was flying between the pillars, the buzz of its wings fading and returning. There was a scent in the still air, sweet, biting. Though the air was still, the scent moved with the bee, strong when it was loud, faint in the bee's faintness.

The wardens stopped at the window, and said:

> "Shick-Shack, oak tree,
> What dost thou see?"

The windows of the north and south aisles were marked with flowers and leaf and seed, one in every diamond pane, two patterns to every window, and a border around. William looked.

"Hollin – Cuckoo Bread – " There were so many he did not know. "Galligaskins – " He twisted in Grandad's hold, and tried to tell. "Jackanapes – Devilberry – Vervey – "

The wardens shook their heads.

"Popple – Robin-run-in-th'Hedge – "

> "Shick-Shack, oak tree,
> What dost thou see?"

"At side!" whispered Grandad.

William looked at the border of the window in front of him.

It was a gold Crown of Glory, against a brown field, with cross-hatching above and below and two small roundels of clear glass in the brown. William started to tremble. He stammered.

> " 'The strongest poison ever known
> Came from Caesar's laurel crown.' "

"Gripe, griffin, hold fast!" Grandad whispered.

"But it's what I wrote!"

About the rim of the crown there ran a wavy line, and in each bend was a single black dot, just as William had drawn under his hand practice.

> "Shick-Shack, oak tree,
> What dost thou see?"

"Gripe, griffin, hold fast!" whispered Grandad again. "They'll ask thee nobbut thrice!"

"Crown – me practice – "

Squarker and Tiddy looked at each other. Tiddy nodded, and they chanted together:

> "Cockle-bread and green wood;
> Man of leaf and golden hood."

William sobbed with the fear and the strain and the not understanding.

"Cockle-bread and green wood;
Man of leaf and golden hood."
"Gripe, griffin, hold fast!"
They willed him. And he saw.

The pattern turned before him, so that what was in was out. The brown was a head formed from leaves of oak, the roundels closed eyes, and nose and mouth and ears the spikes of the crown.

"It's a man! Painted yellow! In a net!"

"Man of leaf and golden hood.
We mun wake him, if we could."

Grandad squeezed William's arm in pleasure and moved him away from the window. The wardens crossed the church to a window of the north wall and pointed to the border.

"Shick-Shack, oak tree,
What dost thou see?"

A gold Crown of Glory against a brown field, with cross-hatching above and below and two small roundels of clear glass, but with dark centres, and a line of the same circles on the rim, just as William had drawn.

"It's him!"

Again, the pattern turned, and what was in was out, but now the eyes were open, staring.

"What's he looking at?"

"Thee? Mebbe?" said Squarker.

"Each morning," said Tiddy, "sun peeps that all's well; and, fetching night, closes to hushabie in his eyes."

"Who is he?" said William.

The buzzing was in his head, and, for a moment, as he looked into those eyes, he was of the bee and the bee was of him, and the scent stifled with its bitter fragrance.

Squarker, Tiddy and Grandad took him back to the south door.

[29]

Squarker and Tiddy stood by either post.

"With right and with might," they shouted. "With skill and with will. Let might help right. And skill go before will. And right before might. So goeth our mill."

"Jack Miller prayeth that thou makest a good end of that thou hast begun," said Tiddy Turnock.

"And dost better and aye better," said Squarker Kennerley. "For, at the even, men heareth the day."

Grandad urged William into the porch, and the door was shut behind them. When they were past the arch of curved trunks, Grandad loosed his grip.

"Well, youth, you said yon nominy champion. Ay. Champion. Grand as owt."

5

The dog was barking on Mutlow.

"Gyp!"

It stood at the trees on the top of the hillock.

"Gyp!"

The dog heard William, but did not come to him. It barked and turned in excitement.

"Dall thy eyes, Gyp, if you're twitting me," said William, and began to climb the slope. The dog leapt up to lick his face when he reached the clump of sycamores.

"What is it, Gyp? Where've you been? What is it, then?" William fondled the ears, and the dog sat with its tongue hanging out, looking at him. Then it lay on the ground. William joined him, squatting on one heel, an arm on his bent knee, the other hand stroking the dog.

"What made you so nowty with Yedart? He didn't mean no harm. But the old youth was right. It wouldn't have done. It puts a quietness on you, does churching. You're frit. But, at after, it puts a quietness."

The dog closed its eyes. William looked out from Mutlow.

It was not a high place, but it fell away in rolling land on every side across the parish and the plain. Hills stood all around. The chain of Shining Tor and Shutlingslow and Sutton and Cloud and Congleton Edge ended at the Old Man of Mow, and, far behind Astbury, there were hills, but he did not know their names. Mountains that his grandfather said were at Wales heaved into the distance. Then

Beeston cliff, High Billinge, Delamere, and, beyond Blackden, there was a flash that he had been told was the sea; but, nearer, Mount Ship, Castle Rock and the Beacon marked the furthest he had been: never ten miles from Mutlow was all his world.

"What's up?"

The dog had lifted its head and was listening. William heard nothing. The dog dropped its head again, but its brow wrinkled as the eyes watched William.

"You daft ha'porth." William chuckled.

A light breeze ruffled the sycamores. The dog watched. William's smile changed to a puzzlement. He turned to look as he caught the faint near wailing of women that had been on the before-dawn wind.

"Now then," he said.

The dog sat up and looked at the tree in front of it.

"No! Bloody no!"

The trunk shimmered with the patterns: the split lights of the barn.

"I said bloody no! You leave me bloody be!"

And he ran down the bank of Mutlow, wild, arms out of control and legs stretched to the brink of falling.

The dog stayed on the hill.

The ground became level, and yet he stumbled, head too far forward, off balance. He blundered through a hedge, and strode a ditch and splashed through Chapel Brook before his limbs were his own again. He made himself walk, yet had to run; but, by the time he reached Tiddy Turnock's farm, he could stop and hold on to the oak for sanctuary. No glimmering shapes would mark that rutted skin. He held the doorway of its clefts until his breath was calm, and then he entered.

He sat on the leaves and hugged his shins. Slowly time came back to him, and he drew his hands across his eyes and down his cheeks.

"By heck."

He looked up through the crown of the tree.

"Cush, cush. Cush-a-cush." A kestrel hovered low.

"Cush, cush, cush. Cush-a-cush."

The kestrel did not move. William stood, trying not to frighten the bird.

"Cush, cush."

The kestrel remained. William climbed up the slope of the inside of the tree. Where the trunk had split, the bark had grown over the lip of the gash, making a banister rail on either side.

"Cush, cush."

He was inside the crown, his head framed by leaves and branches, the kestrel just above him. He reached up his wrist.

"Cush, cush, me beauty."

He kept still, his hand held waiting and the kestrel only inches away. It lowered its claws: and a woman laughed nearby. The kestrel veered. The moment had passed.

William turned around, so that he was sitting in the crown, looking into the trunk. Footsteps approached, and Edward and Esther came into the oak. They stood, each leaning against a separate portion of trunk.

"Well, Esther."

"Well, Yedart."

"Well, Esther?"

"Well, Yedart?"

"You said that you had need to see me."

"Ay."

"On what account?"

"Oh: nowt."

"Nothing?"

"Well, summat and nowt."

"What is it you mean? What do you want of me?"

Esther sat down.

"Here, Yedart, and then."

Edward joined her in the tree.

"So?"

"Have you asked your father if he'll set me on yet?" said Esther.

"I have not had the opportunity."

"Oh, Yedart!"

"He has been in Town; and is only lately back."

"But you said you'd speak for me!"

"I did. And I shall."

"You promised."

"I shall speak for you. But are you not content, so close to William?"

"I want to better meself."

"In what manner?" said Edward.

"I'm fretted with farms, and me old Buckley's whowball; moiling every hour God sends, with him blahting and blasting for me pains. I want to live in a grand house, and look after every kind of beautiful thing you can think of: old things: brass."

Edward laughed affectionately.

"Yay. I do."

"There is but one thing that I have ever wanted," said Edward. "Yet my father will not have it."

"And what's that?"

"The sea. To have a ship under me, and sail the oceans, and to find new worlds. To see strange stars under strange skies. To meet the Anthropophagi, Uroboros, the Laistrygones and all that's wonderful in God's Creation. But my father will not. I am to take Holy Orders, and he has the Living for me. My world is here."

Esther pulled his head over down to her breast. "Then you can set me on, if your father won't! There's grand stuff in a vicarage."

Edward nuzzled up to her, half laughing, half crying. "Oh, Esther! Oh, Het!"

She stroked the back of his neck. "Come, Yedart, come. There. There. Would you still it were a ship under you?"

Esther looked up into the roof of the oak, and her eyes met William's. The set of her face froze and she held his gaze and went on stroking Edward's neck. William did not move as the oak saved him and he entered its eternity, with the wood and the leaves and the bark, and the roots thicker than trees, until eternity was past.

"Up with you, Yedart," said Esther. "Enough now."

Edward tried to kiss her, and pushed himself away, dusted his clothes and left, undignified, without speaking.

William slid down the inside of the trunk and stood over her.

"Why did you?" he whispered. "Why?"

"He's a lad as is not happy," said Esther. "And he means well: mostly."

"Het. Stanleys is fause as foxes."

"Yes, Will."

William lifted Esther to her feet, and they embraced.

"As ring-tailed monkeys. Het."

6

In the dusk, from the glowing oak the split trunk put its shadows across the ground. The red of the centre moved more shadows against the walls of the tree. And there was laughter.

The women of hoodman blind were on their knees about a fire of acorns: Martha, Phoebe, Matty, Betty, Ann, Sarah and Esther. The acorns were a bright hot ash, and over it was a griddle. Each woman was kneading dough, working it on a Kerridge roof slate. They giggled and laughed. Phoebe lifted her head, and sang.

"My granny is sick and now is dead . . . "

"My granny is sick and now is dead," they answered.

"And I'll go mould my cockle-bread . . . "

"And I'll go mould my cockle-bread."

"Up with my heels, and down with my head . . . "

"Up with my heels, and down with my head."

"And this is the way to mould cockle-bread!" They all sang.

The shadows in the tree copied the words, as the chorus went out again.

> "My granny is sick and now is dead,
> And I'll go mould my cockle-bread.
> Up with my heels, and down with my head,
> And this is the way to mould cockle-bread!"

With each singing there was more laughing, and the shadows rolled and rose in a growing surge, faster, as the dark closed about the oak and the fire shone in the brazier of the tree.

"We'll do at that!"

The song fell apart with the speed and the laughter.

"Now then, Het! Let's be having you on the Hamestan!"

Phoebe and Matty took Esther by the hand and led her from the oak. A few yards up the bank, and just in the firelight, a narrow block of gritstone, no more than three feet high, stood from the ground. Whether it was rough-hewn or natural, the top of it was smooth. Esther wore a plain white bodice and a red petticoat.

Phoebe and Matty helped Esther to straddle the stone.

"Eh! It's cold!" Esther shouted in pretended surprise.

"It'll soon be warm!" answered Sarah from the oak.

Matty straightened the petticoat, so that it fell evenly about the stone. Esther's toes just reached the ground.

"Are you set?"

"Ay," said Esther.

Matty called to the women in the oak.

"Ready?"

"Ready!"

"Come on, then!"

"Have you flour enough, Het?"

"Plenty!" said Matty. And she took a handful from her pocket and thrust it up hard under Esther's skirt. Esther shouted again, again pretending.

"Come on!" said Matty. "Don't dally!"

Sarah took two pieces of dough, the shape of pasties, and ran to the stone. She pushed one under Esther, and worked the other in her hands.

"Thrutch!" said Matty.

Esther lifted her feet, bore down on the Hamestan, squirmed, and stood again immediately. Sarah reached for the dough, took it and put the second under Esther.

[37]

"Thrutch!"

Esther bore down, and up. Sarah ran back to the fire and dropped both pieces onto the griddle.

Esther dismounted from the stone.

"Who's the next lucky un?"

Matty sat astride, and Sarah came up with a fresh lump of dough, but only one.

"Thrutch!" said Esther.

Matty bore down, and Sarah ran back to the fire. Phoebe took Matty's place.

"Thrutch!" said Esther.

"Eh up!" Phoebe cried.

"More flour!" said Esther. Matty replenished Phoebe from her pocket.

"Thrutch!"

"And another!"

Sarah followed Phoebe, Ann followed Sarah; and so the women ran backwards and forwards between the oak and the stone, Esther ministering to their comfort with the flour.

"Thrutch! Nay, Betty! Call that cockle-bread? Whatever would Isaac think? Wibble-wabble, woman!"

Until there were eight pieces of dough at the fire, and Esther helped the last rider down from the Hamestan and they went to join the others in the oak.

When the cockle-bread was baked, all the loaves except the first were taken from the griddle, while the first was left until it was black and flames burned blue around. Then Esther flipped it clear into the grass, and, when it was cool enough to hold, she put it with her other loaf and knelt by the fire.

She took earth and skeered the embers. And as she spread the covering, and the light dimmed, Esther sang.

"Acorn cup and oaken tree,
  Bid my true love come to me:
  Between moonlight and firelight,
  Bring him over the hills tonight;
  Over the meadows, over the moor,
  Over the rivers, over the sea,
  Over the threshold and in at the door.
  Acorn cup and oaken tree,
  Bring my true love back to me."

The fire was covered. One by one, the women took their cockle-bread and walked away, Esther leading, carrying the white loaf and the black.

They went to their homes. Some by Knaves' Acre, and Cherry Barrow, some by Katty's Croft and Missick and Big Eels Moss and Little Furry Field; and all singing. "Acorn cup and oaken tree . . . " Some by Blake Low, Laughing Croft. "Bid my true love come to me . . . " By Prison Barr Bank, by Little Sun Field, Black Pit, Middle Cinder Hill. "Between moonlight and firelight . . . " Farther Senichar, Lanthorne Field. And, in every farm and cottage, the women, young and old, turned to their windows and sang. "Bring him over the hills tonight; Over the meadows, over the moor, Over the rivers, over the sea . . . " Across the parish, by Big Mere Heyes, Sing Pool Meadow. "Over the threshold and in at the door . . . " Nick Acre, Little Lowmost, Clover Croft. The whole parish, in the night, all the women, "Bring my true love back to me," the singing.

7

William was wearing his Sunday best. He trimmed the freshly cut bough of oak with a hatchet. The young leaves glowed with a green that hurt. The light was in the leaves.

Edward Stanley rode up the lane to the farm.

"Good day, Will."

"Ay," said William.

"May I see what it is you are about?"

"Ay."

Edward opened his book and began to sketch details of how William worked.

William bound the oak to the gatepost with rope, pulling each turn, so that there was no play between bough and post.

"I have read your hand practice," said Edward.

"Ay."

"It was done well."

"Oh, ay?"

"But have you contemplated what it signifies?"

"It's me practice."

"The words, Will. What do they mean?"

"Me practice."

William tested the bough.

" 'The strongest poison ever known came from Caesar's laurel crown,' " said Edward.

"Ay. I recollect."

"But do you not question?"

"No."

"It says that all men are equal, none beholden to another."

"Oh, ay?"

"They have killed their king in France on that account."

"Ay, well, France."

"And many such of high degree."

"I shouldn't wonder."

William put an extra turn about the post, and tightened the knot. He checked the firmness of the bough once more, and stood back to see that it was upright.

"She'll do," he said. "Be good, Yedart." And he went into the house, leaving Edward. Edward sat for a while, then put the book in his pocket, and rode on.

Esther was in the kitchen. She was wearing an apron over the red petticoat, and the white bodice above. She crumbled bread into a bowl, sprinkled salt over it, and poured hot milk from a pan. She stood at the sideboard and spooned the mess into her mouth.

"No pobs for you today, me lad," she said.

"I don't want none," said William.

He sat at the table, but ate nothing. He took the swaddledidaff from his pocket and turned it in the light.

"You think a lot on that, don't you?" said Esther.

"You give it me," said William.

"But it's nobbut a stone. Yet I've a month's mind you'd rather have that than my china."

"Oh, I would," said William.

"What for?"

"You give it me. And, when you turn it, you can see lights, pictures, all sorts. Yon china's one picture; and it's a rum un."

"It'll wear your britches out," said Esther. "And it's me as'll have to

[41]

mend them – What the dickens is going on? What's he up to now?"

There was shouting in the lane, and a horse galloped away. A dog barked.

The kitchen door was banged open and Grandad came in, his stick under his arm, his eyes glittering, as he crumpled a sheet of paper in his hands and thrust it into the fire. He held it down in the ashes with his stick until the flames died. "Right!" he said.

"Whatever is it?" said Esther.

"What is it?" said Grandad. "I'll tell you what is it! I shall! One of Stanley's gawbies, that's what is it! One of Stanley's gawbies comes riding up, fine as a new scraped carrot, and starts at driving a nail in our gatepost for fixing yon paper. 'And what are you at?' I says to him. 'Oh,' he says, 'Sir John told me.' 'Well,' I says, 'you can tell Sir John it's on fire back; and you'll take that nail with you when you go, out of my gatepost.' 'Oh, shall I?' he says. 'Ay,' I says, 'you shall.' And I ketches him a clinker with me stick aside of his head. 'Oh!' he says. 'Give over!' 'Then you get that nail out,' I says, 'else I'll ketch thee another!' And that were it. Ay! He hoiked out the nail, and away. Ay! I wound his watch for him! What? I did that! I wound his watch!"

He sat in the man's chair. "Eh dear! Dear, dear!" And he mopped the tears of laughter with his neck cloth. "Now hadn't you ought get yourselves fettled?"

"We're ready," said Esther, and took off her apron.

William put the swaddledidaff in his pocket.

Grandad went with them as far as the gate. He looked at the post, trying to find the nail hole. Then he grasped the oak bough and tested its firmness. "You've done a grand job there, youth," he said.

"Heel, Gyp," said William.

"Be good, and then," said Grandad.

Esther took William's hand. They walked off down the lane, the dog following.

"Ay. Be good," said Grandad, and looked again for trace of the nail.

"There's bits everywhere," said Esther. "What's it for?"

"Yay," said William.

"See at them. They're all over."

"What?"

"There's paper stuck all over."

"Oh, ay."

Every house had its bough of green, at gate or gable or window or door. And on the posts and the hedge trees there were sheets of paper fastened.

"There's writing."

"Sarn it, Het! Hush up, can't you?"

"Suit yourself," said Esther. "They weren't there before, and that's a fact."

They came to the oak.

The men of hoodman blind were waiting in the tree. The dead fire had been spread out and pieces of charcoal sorted from the ashes. The men had blackened their faces with the charcoal, and were wearing harness bells tied below the knee, and holding the two halves of a flail. Two branches, the length of William, had been wrenched from the oak and laid against the trunk. Edward Stanley stood, in his normal dress, and clean faced, making notes. No one spoke.

Esther let go of William, and he went and sat on a root.

Niggy Bower took a knob of charcoal, spat into his hand, rubbed the charcoal in the spit and began to daub William's face. He blackened where he touched: the eyes and ears and neck were harshly white. When that was done, he tied bells below William's knees and stepped back.

Esther reached inside her bodice and pulled out the ground net. She went forward and cast the net over William and rolled it to form a halter, holding him by the two ends around his neck. Niggy lifted the big branches and gave them to William, one in each hand, so that his body was covered with leaves and his face framed by them. Esther pulled gently on the net, and William stood up, and Esther sang.

"I'll dye, I'll dye my petticoat red;
For the lad I love I'd bake my bread;
And then my daddy would wish that I were dead.
Sweet Willy in the morning among the rush."

The men started to knock their flail halves together in time, and processed out of the tree, Esther and William going before them. They moved with a hopping, stamping tread, everyone but William singing, and Esther leading, dancing backwards, with the net.

"Shoorly, shoorly, shoo-gang-rowl!
Shoo-gang-lolly-mog, shoog-a-gang-a-low!
Sweet Willy in the morning among the rush!"

They danced away. Edward mounted and rode after, past a horseman wearing Stanley livery who had been watching. The horseman touched his forehead to Edward and walked the horse towards the oak. Edward nodded in reply. The horseman took a sheet of rolled paper from a pouch, opened it and nailed it with a hammer to the tree. Edward hesitated.

" – Sweet Willy in the morning among the rush!"

Edward turned, and followed the dancers.

"I'll dye, I'll dye my petticoat red;
For the lad I love I'd bake my bread;
And then my daddy would wish that I were dead –"

The dog gambolled round, backwards and forwards; gambolled, and herded.

" – Sweet Willy in the morning among the rush."

They danced towards the church on its mound. The belfry door was open, and on the shingled spire, below the yellow painted weathercock, was fastened a branch of green oak.

> "Shoorly, shoorly, shoo-gang-rowl!
> Shoo-gang-lolly-mog, shoog-a-gang-a-low!
> Sweet Willy in the morning among the rush!"

As they reached the belfry, the door was slammed shut against them from within.

The dance ended. The dog sat apart.

The men went to the door and banged rhythmically upon it with the butt ends of their flails, chanting.

> "Open the way and let us in!
> We have your favour for to win!
> Whether we sit, stand or fall,
> We'll do our best to please you all!"

The two church wardens, with their staffs, opened the door, and the dancers entered. The door closed; and the dog lay down.

The belfry was a frame of huge timbers, like the trunk of the oak, as big as the oak, but pegged and jointed from its root to the dark narrowing of the spire above; and it held them all about.

The vicar, in his robes, stood in the open doorway to the nave. He said:

> "Who stands in the belfry tree?
> What have you to do with me?"

William drew his breath and spoke all in one tone.

> "Here comes Shick-Shack who has never been It,
> With my big head and little wit."

"Where have you been, Shick-Shack?" said the vicar.

> "Through Hickety-Pickety, France and High Spain,
> Three shitten shippons, o'er three laughing
> doorsteps,
> And now I have come back to England again."

"What have you fetched, Shick-Shack?"

"I've a pill in my pocket to cure all ill:
  Time gone, time yet and time that will."
"Enter in, Shick-Shack," said the vicar,
"With those at your back."

The vicar turned and led the way into the nave.

The church was full, everyone standing. The pews had been taken out to make more room, with only the middle of the nave clear to the altar.

There were Buckleys and Rathbones, Slaters, Edges, Sims; Masseys and Thorleys, Barns, Bowers, Beswicks, Lathams, and Birtles. All the parish, filling the aisles, up against the walls, children on shoulders, blocking the windows, crowding the gallery so that the band could hardly play. There were Lawtons and Stubbs and Leas, Worthingtons, Mottersheads, and Baileys. Boys and youths sitting on the windbraces of the roof arches and the boughs of the pillars, making the church one people.

Esther followed the vicar, walking backwards, leading William by the net. Edward Stanley could not find space, and stood at the belfry door, peering where he was able.

The women of hoodman blind were sitting in the north choir stalls, every one holding her cockle-bread. The altar cloth was scarlet and sewn about with oak leaves of gold wire.

The vicar paused at the font, which had water in it, and on the rim of the font lay a twig of oak. Esther and William stood, the men behind them. The vicar dipped the green twig in the font and shook the water over William and said:

"Gently dip,
  But not too deep,
  For fear you make the golden bird to weep."

He put the twig back on the rim and faced the altar. The men formed a file, a flail handle on each shoulder. The vicar headed the procession up the aisle, singing.

"Fair maiden, white and red – "

" – Comb me smooth and stroke my head," the people responded.

" – And thou shalt have some cockle-bread," sang the vicar.

"And every hair a sheaf shall be – "

" – And every sheaf a golden tree."

They entered the chancel, and the men went to their places in the south choir stalls: Joshua, John, Charlie, Elijah, Sam, Isaac, Niggy.

Esther led William to stand at the end of the communion rail, while she stood on his left, still holding the net, and facing east.

The vicar went to the other side of the rail and closed it behind him. He bent his knee to the altar, then took the branches from William and placed them on the altar one at a time. He took the net, and put it with the branches.

William knelt at the rail. The women came from the choir stalls, in line beside Esther, and they all knelt.

The vicar lifted a paten from the altar, and on it were two loaves of the cockle-bread: one white, and one charred black. The vicar spoke to William.

"Have you come filled, or have you come fasting?"

"I have come fasting."

"Which will you take: the burnt bread with God's blessing, or the white bread with God's curse?"

"The burnt bread with God's blessing," said William.

He held his hands cupped, and the vicar put the black loaf into them. William broke the bread, and it snapped as crumbs and lumps of cinder, which he began to eat. The edges cut his mouth and he tried not to gag on the dust as he chewed. He had no spit to soften the hardness, and the dry flakes stuck and burned in his throat when he swallowed. Each mouthful was more bitter than the one before, and he could not keep the tears from his eyes.

The vicar put his right hand on William's head.

"The morning star, O Mary, to the bird of the bright wing.

"The rainbow, O Mary, to the shining bird.

" 'My son, eat thou honey, because it is good; and the honeycomb which is sweet to thy taste. So shall the knowledge of wisdom be unto thy soul: when thou hast found it, then there shall be a reward, and thy expectation shall not be cut off.' "

The vicar moved to Esther and gave her the white loaf, and said: "Esther. Take, and be fruitful." And so he went along the line of the women, who held up their cockle-bread in turn to be blessed on the paten. "Betty. Take, and be fruitful. Martha. Take, and be fruitful. Ann. Take, and be fruitful. Phoebe. Take, and be fruitful. Sarah. Take, and be fruitful. Martha. Take, and be fruitful."

After the blessing, the women went back to the choir stalls and Esther with them. William gulped at the last brutal crust, and joined the men. The vicar put the paten on the altar, bent his knee, and faced the church. He made the sign of the cross.

"The bee, O Mary, to the bird of gold."

William choked, but Niggy thumped his back.

The vicar climbed the steps into the pulpit. He tucked his hands into his sleeves, and spoke.

" 'And they saw a tall tree by the side of the river, one half of which was in flame from the root to the top, and the other half was green and in full leaf.' Hear, too, what Isaiah saith: 'And the Lord have removed men far away, and there be a great forsaking 'n the land. But yet in it shall be a tenth, and it shall return, and shall be eaten: as a teil tree, and as an oak.' And also it is written: 'And on either side of the river was there the tree of life, which bare twelve manner of fruits, and yielded her fruit every month: and the leaves of the tree were for the healing of the nations.' "

"Gerrit down thee!" whispered Niggy to William.

"Dearly beloved. This day we hold sacred the custom long hallowed in this parish, whereby all that are brought as infants to this House of Oak to be received into Christ's Church, shall, when they be of mature years, return, and, by tokens of sacrifice and charity, give thanks for the renewal of life and the promise of life everlasting made manifest in these His Creatures of branch and bread – "

There was a hammering of metal on the belfry door, but the vicar continued.

" – so that we may partake of the fruits of the earth and the sanctified pleasures of the flesh, rejoicing in the knowledge that – "

He could not go on. The people were restless, looking to the back of the church; and Tiddy Turnock and Squarker Kennerley were already advancing on the belfry with their staffs. But, before they reached the end of the nave, the hammering stopped and the door was pushed open. The morning light glared on a sheet of paper that had been nailed to the door, and a man in Stanley livery stepped back to allow another in. This one was dressed in a coat of brocaded silk, and he gave his hat to the man at the door without looking at him, and entered the church.

The people were silent, and the man's footsteps were loud on the stone floor. He walked with purpose, towards the chancel, acknowledging nobody.

Behind him, five others, all but one liveried, came into the belfry. Edward Stanley hung back.

"Sir John?" said the vicar as the man reached the pulpit; but he walked into the chancel and stopped.

"Buckley."

He spoke without heat or question, but as a claim. William stood in the choir: he had no thought or choice.

"Cuff that man."

Grandad got to his feet at the back of the church as the six followers entered. "Now then!"

"Sir – " said Edward.

"Cuff him."

Sam Slack, the constable, moved forward with no haste. "Come on, youth," he said. "You're summonsed." He held out a pair of hand-cuffs.

"I am never!" said William.

"Yay, but you are. Come along, now, there's a good lad."

"What for?"

"Sir John says."

" 'Sir John says!' " cried Grandad. "I've known yon since his bum were as big as me shirt button! 'Sir John says!' That's no law!" His neighbours held him. The church was filled with whispers and the noise of women afraid.

"Father – " said Edward, from the door of the nave.

"Cuff him, constable."

"As heck as like!"

William jumped the communion rail and seized one of the oak branches and held it before him. Sam Slack stepped backwards. John Stanley motioned his men with his head. They came to the chancel steps.

"Sir John!" said the vicar.

"Remain in your clack-loft, parson."

"This is sacrilege, Sir John!"

"And this is lewdness and Popery, sir; if you will have it."

The men closed in, and William came over the rail to meet them, the branch raised as a club.

"I'll bloody kill you!"

"No, Will," said Esther. "It's them as'll kill you."

"I'll do for the lot on 'em! I bloody shall!"

The white skin in the black made his panicked eyes seem bigger, and even the men hesitated before his advance.

"I bloody shall! I bloody − ! I bloody − !"

He stopped. The bough quivered above his head.

"Bunj-i-i-i-l!!"

He threw the branch high in the air and caught it and whirled it about him, from hand to hand; and, in the whirling, William danced, mocking, taunting, defiant, unafraid before the men, turning his back on them as he leaped high, facing them as he crouched, mouth open, nostrils flared, whooping and howling, and from his mouth came words.

"Mulla-mullung mulla-mullung Tharangalkbek! Goomah! Goomah! Goomah! Minggah! Minggah! Minggah! Thundal!"

"He speaks in tongues!" said the vicar.

The men drew together, uncertain. Children cried.

"He is a clown that gibbers, and is lunatic," said Stanley.

"No, Sir John. Does not Saint Paul say: 'He that speaketh in an unknown tongue, speaketh not unto men, but unto God: for no man understandeth him; howbeit in the spirit he speaketh mysteries'?"

"I say that he is lunatic."

"Tundun! Binbeal!" declaimed William. "Thuroongarong! Neeyangarra! Murrangurk!"

John Stanley held out his hand behind him, and one of his men put a pistol, ready primed, into it.

"Then let him speak unto God."

He walked forward to where William danced and pointed the pistol at him. William stopped, and held the branch, not as a club, but as a spear. His mouth was a gash in his black face.

Esther came from the choir, set herself between Stanley and William and took hold of the branch.

"Give us it."

William looked at her, and frowned.

[51]

"Purranmurnin," he said.

"Give us it. Come on, love. You can't do nowt."

"Tallarwurnin."

"Give us the branch."

William opened his hands. He was silent. Then:

"I have been dead before."

Squarker Kennerley looked across at Tiddy Turnock. "Eh heck." He raised his staff. "Hallelujah! Shick-Shack!"

Tiddy raised his staff. He turned to the people.

"Yay! Hosanna, and all!"

"Shick-Shack!" The voice of the people made the timbers of the church boom. "Shick-Shack! Shick-Shack! Shick-Shack! Hallelujah!"

At once, William sagged; the grace and arrogance were gone. "Het. Don't leave me."

"Come on, love."

Esther led him to Sam Slack, and the cuffs were put about his wrists and the men took him. John Stanley returned the pistol.

"Yet he did speak in tongues," said the vicar.

Esther rounded on John Stanley.

"My thanks to you – Cumberbach?"

"Esther Cumberbach. Sir. Now! What's up with you? What the holy buggery is up?"

"Whose hand is this?" said John Stanley. He took a paper from his pocket and held it in front of William.

"It's me practice," said William.

"Did you write this?"

"Ay."

"Sir!" said Edward. "That was in my chamber!"

"And how should I not know it?"

"Sir!"

"By the God!" said Grandad. "The youth's done nowt wrong!"

."This not wrong?" said Stanley. " 'The strongest poison ever known came from Caesar's laurel crown.' 'Ancient abuses are not by their antiquity converted into virtues.' 'Man has rights which no statutes or usages take away.' This Jacobin treason not wrong? What, then, may be right?"

"You talk like a pig piddles!" shouted Grandad.

"It was me practice," said William.

"The man does not comprehend!" said Edward.

"It was me practice: for writing," said William. "What's he on at, Het?"

"He writes, and does not comprehend?" said Stanley. "Let him comprehend me this." He held out his hand to the man who had nailed the paper to the church door. The man gave him another, rolled up, which Stanley passed to William. William struggled in the cuffs to unroll the paper.

"What is it?" he said.

"Read," said Stanley. "It would seem that you are able. And let all hear."

William read aloud, hesitating.

" 'Any person lopping oak trees for the ridiculous custom of decorating houses on May the twenty-ninth will be prosecuted under the recent Act which allows transportation for life for such an offence. J. T. Stanley'."

There was a murmur of anger through the church.

"You read well," said Stanley. "But do you comprehend?"

"What does he mean?" said William.

"How may he comprehend, sir?" said Edward. "The man has little use of words!"

"Yet comprehend or no," said Stanley, "my oaks were lopped, though I have had this intelligence posted throughout the parish, where all may see."

[53]

"Few can read!" said Edward.

"I don't know what he means, Het!" said William. "All them words!"

"He means, Buckley, that you may take your tracts with you to New Holland, and entertain and plot with your fellow Jacobins and Levellers to your heart's delight. And I wish you God's speed."

"Sir John," said the vicar. "The man is plainly innocent."

"The oaks are on your altar, sir. Remove him."

The men marched William towards the belfry. When he reached Grandad he put his shackled arms over the old man's head and neck, embracing him.

"I'll be back, Grandad, never fret."

The old man was crying.

"My song, youth. Fair wind to your arse and a bottle of moss." Charcoal was smudged on his cheek.

The men took possession again. Esther stood mute on the chancel steps.

John Stanley paused at the font and picked up the twig of oak and crumpled it between his fingers and dropped it to the floor. He spoke to the vicar. "Here's a thought your teeth should clench: all green comes to withering."

Helpless shouts began. The people were trying to move among the pillared trunks of the nave, under the curved bracing, the limbs of the roof, lost in a wood. The vicar strove to restore them.

"Hear what our Lord saith!

" 'Blessed are they which are persecuted for righteousness' sake: for theirs is the kingdom of heaven.

" 'Blessed are ye, when men shall revile you and persecute you, and shall say all manner of evil against you falsely, for my sake − ' "

The church emptied of Stanley, and the people responded to the vicar and his words in that place. They knelt. Esther remained, looking to the door.

" 'Ye are the salt of the earth — ' "

As he passed from the belfry, William turned his head over his shoulder to Esther at the chancel steps. Framed in the arches of oak she stood, and their eyes became their memory along the separation of the church.

" 'Let your light so shine before men — ' "

"Het! I'll be back for you! I promise!"

" 'Think not that I come to destroy the law, or the prophets: I am not come to destroy, but to fulfil.' "

William was flung onto the mound. The dog watched. "Gyp! Seize 'em! Seize 'em!"

The dog flattened its ears, and lay still.

Alone in the belfry, Edward blocked his father's path.

"The man is innocent, sir."

"He writes. The example is to be made. And my oaks are lopped."

"This darkness must end."

"Gyp — !!"

"They shall not write."

II

CRANK CUFFIN

And þer he festnes þe fete and fathmez aboute,
And stod vp in his stomak þat stank as þe deuel.
þer in saym and in sorȝe þat sauoured as helle,
þer watz bylded his bour þat wyl no bale suffer

"Patience"
lines 273/6

8

"I chases 'em. I flaps my apron at 'em. But they sees me coming. They sees my apron. But I'll get 'em, one day."

" ' – her black joke and belly so white, so white; her black joke and her belly so white!' "

Oh, give over.

"We was flying a blue pigeon; but before we can bite the ken, some mollisher whiddles beef, and I'm bummed and naps fourteen penn'orth."

Across the deck, forrard. Too dark.

"The cove's so scaly, he'd spice a mawkin for his jasey."

Not his jasey. Never. It were his weskit.

"Shema yisroel, a-don-ai elo-henu, a-donai echod."

"Mother of God! Who's the porker?"

"The Geordie Smous kid."

"Chelsea College to a sentry box, there'll be indorsing dues concerned!"

Give over!

"How long shall us be on the Herring-Pond?"

"Six month, within ames ace."

"Somewhat more than three days and nights in the belly of this whale, I fear."

That's a nob! What's he at?

"Not entirely star-crossed in his solitude, was Jonas; before St Giles's Greek was noised."

STRANDLOPER

Who is he?

"Aye aye! There'll be indorsing dues concerned."

"I chases 'em. I flaps my apron at 'em. But they sees me coming. They sees my apron. But I'll get 'em, one day."

"Come on, mates! Bear a bob!

> " 'Oh, we are the boys of the Holy Ground,
> And we'll dance upon nothing, and turn us
> around.
> We'll dance upon nothing and turn us around;
> For we are the boys of the Holy Ground!' "

"I chases 'em. I flaps my apron at 'em. But they sees me coming. They sees my apron. But I'll get 'em, one day."

"Oi! You! Jaw-me-dead!"

"It's lag fever."

"His garret's unfurnished."

"I'll hush the cull, if he don't stubble it. Bloody end to me if I don't."

"I chases 'em."

"Bloody end to me! Shut your bone box, lobcock!"

"Hey, Teddy-me-Godson."

"I flaps my apron at 'em."

"Teddy-me-Godson: couch a hogshead, now. Go box the Jesuit and get cockroaches, eh? Mount a corporal and four. That'll put you in fine twig."

"Shema yisroel, a-don-ai elo-henu, a-donai echod."

"Ave Maria, gratia plena, Dominus tecum – "

"But they sees me coming. They sees my apron."

"Vater unser, der du bist im Himmel – "

Sarn it! What's to do wi' 'em? Why don't they shurrup, yowking?

" – ora pro nobis ora pro nobis ora pro nobis ora pro nobis ora – "

Dall yer eyes! Barm pots! All on yer! Talk sense! Or else! Or else! Or else – !

[60]

"We'll dance upon nothing, and turn us around."
　　　　You make the golden bird to weep.
"Shema yisroel, a-don-ai elo-henu, a-donai echod."
"Unser täglich Brot gib uns heute."
"But I'll get 'em – "
" – pro nobis peccatoribus – "
"For we are the boys of the Holy Ground."
" – in hora mortis nostrae."
　　　　　　　　"Kiminary keemo,
　　　　　　　　Kiminary keemo,
　　　　　　　　Kiminary kiltikary, kiminary keemo – "
" – one day."
"Het!"

9

William unlashed his hammock and slung it from the beam. The irons around his wrists were linked by a chain, and, from the chain, a chain went down to the chain that joined the irons at his ankles, and from his right leg a loose, heavy chain lay along the deck. He bent forward and balanced into his hammock, then, with his fettered hands, pulled the loose chain up to him.

"Why is it me as is double slanged?" said William.

"All on account of you're a big, bastardly gullion," said Renter.

"But Jeremiah doesn't scour no darbies at all."

"Ah, that's all on account of the Gorger's a swell, and full of binnacle words and no bear-garden jaw."

"It is more that I would not mutiny, than that my station is preferred," said Jeremiah.

"Binnacles!"

"What was you lagged for, then?" said Eggy Mo.

"I was an attorney at law," said Jeremiah, "who had the misfortune to be unable to account for a banker's draft to the sum of two hundred and nine pounds and seven shillings made out to my senior. I also suffered the misfortune to be found protecting his gold watch. For the which, I am to enjoy a southern clime throughout the next fourteen years."

"And me, I'm served cramp words just for prigging a woolbird!" said Eggy Mo. "How comes you naps only fourteen penn'orth?"

"It must be that I shared your happiness in a more lenient judge at appeal," said Jeremiah.

"Still, I naps a bellowser, not you," said Eggy Mo.

"Life, or fourteen," said Jeremiah: "who is to debate the outcome, whither we are bound?"

"Still," said Eggy Mo, "I reckon two hundred odd quid and a ridge montra beats one old woolbird as was rig-welted."

"I chases 'em. I flaps my apron at 'em. But they sees me coming. They sees my apron. But I'll get 'em, one day."

"I've slept in these slangs more nights than enough," said William. "And they're biting in, what's more."

"Piss on it," said Renter. "I pisses on mine. It hardens 'em off; and they'll not fester."

" 'Rig-welted,' " said Jeremiah. " 'Rig-welted'. Mr Pye, what may this 'rig-welted' mean?"

"It's when a sheep," said Eggy Mo, "same as it's on it back and can't get up."

"That's rean-wawted," said William.

"It's rig-welted."

"Rean-wawted."

"It's casted," said Renter.

"Rean-wawted!"

"Rig-welted!"

"Casted."

"Anyroad, it's stuck," said William.

" 'Therefore is the name of it called Babel; because the Lord did there confound the language of all the earth.' " said Jeremiah. "Gentlemen, it would seem that your St Giles's Greek has some purpose whereby you may commune without bloodletting amongst yourselves at least."

"Casted."

"Rig-welted."

"Give over with your mither," said William. "I can't hear."

He fingered the beam and put his ear to the wood.

"And why should you be a-grinning like a Cheshire cat?" said Renter.

"I'm going home," said William. "It's taking me. It says."

Jeremiah laughed. "A palpable Argo! Yet I must own that it is bound for no Aeëtes' realm, no Colchis, this; and no dusky Medea will proffer you a Golden Fleece, Mr Buckley. To have set an oracular plank from the oak of Dedonal Zeus, on such a ship, is indicative of folly, even in Athena."

"Oh, you and your mollocking," said William. "Talk like a Christian, can't you?"

"He's a rum duke," said Renter.

William stroked the swaddledidaff against his cheek with the other hand.

"Cush, cush. Cush-a-cush."

"Mr Buckley," said Jeremiah, "are you quite well?"

"Ay. Grand as owt."

"But you are not going home. This vessel is bound for New Holland, as you do know."

"Or Van Demon's Land," said Renter.

"I'm going home; and that's a fact."

"Then how, pray?" said Jeremiah.

"Walk. I've been asking the Patlanders. They know."

"Patlanders?" said Renter. "Ar, they would, wouldn't they just? Nigmenog, every Jack-rag of them."

"Eh! Pad!" William shouted.

"What?" answered a voice from the darkness.

"Come here!"

"What for?"

"Me mates don't believe us!"

There was a thump onto the deck, and the chink of leg irons as someone shuffled forward.

"What is it you want?" said the man.

"Tell me mates here how we're getting home."

"On our hocks; how else?"

"Have you perused a globe?" said Jeremiah.

"And what's that?" said Pad.

"Tell 'em," said William.

"Well," said Pad, "it's good as caz. You go north from Port Jackson till you get to this river. The other side's China, and you'll find them that are there are blue."

"They are. I've seen a picture," said Willam. "There's a bridge, and a feller with a boat."

"China," said Pad. "And then you turn left and straight home."

"There's trees," said William. "Two are big uns. You can't miss 'em."

"How shall you know North?" said Jeremiah.

"I've a compass," said Pad.

"But can you read it?" said Jeremiah.

"Read it? And didn't I make it meself?" said Pad. And he hobbled back into the dark.

"And didn't I tell you?" said Renter. "I'd not trust that one's arse with a fart."

10

" 'It is therefore ordered and adjudged by this Court, that you be transported upon the seas, beyond the seas – ' " William looked out through a crack in the closed dead-light. " ' – to such a place as His Majesty, by the advice of His Privy Council, shall think fit to direct and appoint, for the term of your natural life.' "

"Your memory is good," said Jeremiah, from beneath.

"You don't forget," said William. "They put a quietness on you, do them words. 'Upon the seas, beyond the seas.' It's just I never thought as how there'd be so much."

"Ay," said Renter, "and a lot of it's wet."

"It'll take some getting round," said William. "And the sky's looking black aback of Bill's mother's."

"You'd best come on down, then," said Renter. "The chairs are talking."

William crouched along the gloom of the gun deck to the companion ladder and into the dark of the orlop and its air festered with slough and staled blood. He found his hammock and hauled his chain up.

"William?" said Jeremiah.

"What?"

"Suppose: now let us, for the sake of discourse, suppose that Fortune were not to smile on you. Let us suppose that New Holland were to be your domicile, in truth, for the rest of your natural life."

"But I'm going home."

"I said the chairs were talking. It'll be tables next," said Renter.

"I'm feeling badly," said Eggy Mo.

"They're doing some running aloft, by the sound of it," said Renter.

A chair fell over, and the tables began to slide.

"Seun agus saor agus – "

"Nay, Sawney!" shouted William. "Don't you start! Else you'll have 'em all yowking!"

" – Le gaotha caona, caomha, coistre, cubre – "

"Sawney! Be told!"

"Leave him," said Renter. "Sawney knows his boats. And if he's praying, I think I just might try."

A crag of water hit the side of the ship. Sea cascaded down the companion.

"Batten all hatches!" cried a distant voice, and the decks thudded into black.

"Open up!" Eggy Mo screamed. "I'll not drown! You'll not let us! You'll not drown us! Open up!"

"And is it you'll be teaching iron to swim?" shouted Pad.

Eggy Mo was sick into his hammock, coughing and weeping. "I want me Mam."

"And don't we all?" said Pad.

Another sea swept the ship, and water dripped and trickled from the gun deck above. Crying began, both women and men, and the sound of retching. Shouts went up.

William put out his manacled hands in the darkness, balancing the hammock, until he reached Eggy Mo. Tender, so as not to capsize himself, he worked his way to Eggy's hand, which gripped his in spasm.

"Come here, youth," said William, "and I'll tell thee a tale."

"Will you?" said Eggy Mo.

"Once upon a time," said William, "though it weren't in my time, and it weren't in your time, and it weren't in anybody else's time,

Jack and his mother were living on a common – "

"Where is me Mam?" said Eggy Mo.

"She'll be here presently," said William. "Anyroad, they were living on this common in a tumbledown house of sorts, with nobbut a white cow to keep them."

"Wasn't it a brown un?" said Eggy Mo.

"No. I'm telling you. It were white."

"Ay, white," said Renter.

People were blundering about in the wallow and dark, their chains splashing in the water that was gathering on the deck as they tried to find the ladder. Table and chairs were knocked over, and the cries of those who had fallen and could not get to their feet became panic.

"Stay in your hammocks!" shouted William. "You'll be all right! Anyroad, 'Oh,' says the man, 'I'll give you more than you'll get at the market. If you'll sell me your white cow, I'll give you five beans.' "

"Three," said Renter.

"No, they were never," said William.

"Three."

"Oh no they were not! I know how many beans make five!"

" 'Infandum, regina, iubes renovare dolorem.' " said Jeremiah.

"You what?" William nearly lost his balance. "What are you at?"

"Assimilating the disgorgement and crepitation of others while en route for the Antipodes at His Majesty's Pleasure," said Jeremiah, "and assaying to improve on the Bedlam about me. Cows and beans, my dear fellow, cows and beans? When we may founder? Cows and beans!"

"What was it you said?"

"Words that appeared to be appropriate to our situation: no more."

"What's it mean?"

" 'O queen, you bid me relate unspeakable distress.' "

"Is there any more?"

"Much, much more."

"What's it about?"

"It concerns a man who sails from home to find a foreign land."

"Let's hear it."

"It is over long," said Jeremiah, "and I find it somewhat tedious."

"Learn me!" said William. "You must learn me that whateveritis!"

"Teach Latin? Amongst this canting crew? But why not?" said Jeremiah. "And an acquaintance with the language, in particular with an ability to read the first verse of the Fifty-first Psalm, whence its vulgar sobriquet of 'Neck Verse', brings with it the singular advantage of escaping the full rigours of those offences that are held to be capital, as I have good cause to know. Yes, you shall learn your Latin, William. There are worse things to be done with fourteen years."

"No," said William. "You must do it in a sixmonth. I'm going home."

"Then you may as well remain with cows and beans. Cows and beans, William, cows and beans."

The ship pitched under the seas, and the cries in the dark spread along the deck, swearing, pleading, praying and wordless. Only the Irish kept calm, with an unbroken jig of spoons and mouth music. William comforted Eggy Mo.

" – No sooner done than in come the giant, and a great hairy chap he were, by all accounts."

"And what does he say?" said Eggy Mo.

"He says:

'Fee! Fi! Fo! Fum!
I smell the blood of an Englishman!
Be he alive, or be he dead,
I'll grind his bones to make my bread!' "

"By all the Saints!" shouted Pad. "He'd be the great one for a political organisation!"

The hatch was thrown open and there was a rushing of feet on the ladders, and an escort of sailors carrying torches, and of marines with bayonets fixed, pushed the crowd to the sides, leaving a passage clear. Along the gangway came a lieutenant, and with him the chaplain, holding a lantern. The clothes of them all trailed water.

"Aha," said Renter. "Here comes Bobby Knoppy."

"Is all well, Mr Erbin?" said the chaplain to Jeremiah.

"By no means, Mr Knopwood," said Jeremiah. "The people fear for their lives. They are persuaded that the ship will sink."

The check that the sudden occupation had brought became panic again, and the marines had to use the butts of their flintlocks in the closed space.

"Silence!" ordered the lieutenant. "Silence!" His voice cracked.

"He says hush up!" shouted William.

The noise and the groaning subsided. The Irish continued a muted music. They were sitting on their tables, their weight keeping them steady.

"Hush up, Pad," said William.

"Diddle-i-di-di-di, di-diddle-i-diddle-i-diddle-i-di," Pad sang, smiling.

"Listen to the parson!" said William.

The deck was silent for a moment. In the light, those who had fallen were helped to stand.

The chaplain looked William in the eye. William held his gaze.

"Name?" said the lieutenant.

"William Buckley."

"Say 'sir' to the chaplain."

"Me grandad always told me as 'sir' was a poor word for a fool," said William.

The chaplain laughed. "Why is this man double ironed, Mr Johnson?" he said.

"I don't know, sir," said the lieutenant.

"Then do me the honour of discovering the cause."

"Yes, sir. Sergeant!"

"Sir!"

"Take charge."

"Sir!"

The lieutenant ran up the ladder.

"Your grandsire's wisdom," said the chaplain to William, "will, I fear, strain my composure on the voyage." He turned to face the prison deck. "Now! If you heathen, lero lero bullen a-la Teigues will cease from your papist pratings for a moment, I have news for you all. There is a storm, but I have been in worse. And the ship is of His Majesty's line, and not one of your transports that should never lose sight of the Thames."

"But is it the storm that knows it? Sir?" said Pad. "And it's not you, like a rat in a trap. Sir."

"It is my intention to be with you till the storm abate," said the chaplain. "And, if you will give us leave to say a prayer in peace, I shall offer you and your fellows what succour I may or that you will allow."

"You're on. Sir." said Pad.

The lieutenant came back down the ladder and spoke in the chaplain's ear.

"Indeed?" said the chaplain, and looked again at William. "The lieutenant has it from the Captain, Buckley, that, although you be charged with no offence other than that that brought you here, there is a note in the Captain's Orders from the highest office of the Admiralty that you be confined in double irons for the duration of this voyage. Tell me: how may the matter stand thus?"

"That devil wants me dead," said William.

"I recognise no authority," said the chaplain, "other than God Almighty, and through His servant George our King, and His Archbishop. Mr Johnson. Have removed all but the leg irons.

[71]

On the instant."

"Yes, sir," said the lieutenant. "Sergeant, have this man taken up and unmanacle him."

"No," said William. "Thee hold thy water. He thinks as I can't do it. I'll bloody show him. Leave them irons be."

"Pride, William," said Jeremiah. " 'The mouth of the foolish is a rod of pride.' "

"No," said William. "It's him or me."

"Who?"

"Never you mind. I know. Leave them slangs."

"I cannot command you," said the chaplain.

"No, you can't," said William.

"Mr Knopwood," said Jeremiah, "is the ship equipped with slates and pencils that we may use?"

"You have but to ask," said the chaplain. "And now let us proceed, if we may. Mr Johnson. Do me the honour of going to my cabin and bringing me the bottle of brandy wine that you will find there. And then I should be gratified if you and your men were to retire."

"Sir, I may not leave you among the convicts without a guard!"

"To supplicate our Father with flintlock and steel would be a blasphemy, sir," said the chaplain. "Let us not dispute."

"But your life – "

"Is in God's hands. And I would have the brandy in mine."

The lieutenant saluted, returned with the bottle, and withdrew his men. The chaplain stood alone in the pool of lantern light, in the stench and the darkness, feet apart against the roll of the ship, head bent under the beams.

"Let us go to our hammocks, and address ourselves to that Power that rules the heavens, the seas and the dry land."

There was shrieking and spewing and the rattle of chains, but at last even the Irish settled.

[72]

The chaplain began to pray.

"Thou, O Lord, that stillest the raging of the sea, hear, hear us, and save us that we perish not."

"I chases 'em."

"O blessed Saviour, that didst save thy disciples ready to perish in a storm, hear us, and save us, we beseech Thee.

"Lord, have mercy upon us."

"I flaps my apron at 'em."

"Christ, have mercy upon us."

"But they sees me coming."

"Lord, have mercy upon us.

"O Lord, hear us."

"They sees my apron."

"O Christ, hear us."

"God the Father, God the Son, God the Holy Ghost, have mercy upon us, save us now and evermore. Amen."

The lantern swung shadows at the blessing.

"But I'll get 'em, one day."

"Amen."

The chaplain went to the hammock and looked in.

"What is wrong with this man?"

"It's lag fever, sir. He means no harm."

"He was rocked in a stone kitchen, sir."

The chaplain uncorked the bottle and wetted the lips with brandy.

"Here, my lad. This'll bring back your dossity."

"But I'll get 'em, one day."

The chaplain went from hammock to hammock, giving comfort and prayer, ignoring the curses, until he came to the Irish. Only Pad now sat on a table. The rest had gone to their hammocks and were lying with their faces turned away. The chaplain sat on the table, across from Pad, with the lantern and the brandy bottle between them.

"Now, McAllenan, is there anything a Protestant bug can do to help a heathen Teigue?"

"You have me name, sir!"

"I have more than your name. I have your character."

"Well, well, sir. There's a thing."

"What can I do for you? Will you pray with me?"

Pad rummaged in his hammock and brought out a lump of bread and a lump of cheese, both dusted green with mould. He put them on the table.

"If it's not too much trouble, sir, you can flick us some pannam and caz."

The chaplain took a penknife from his pocket and cut a slice from each lump. He gave the bread to Pad.

"The Body of our Lord Jesus Christ, which was given for thee, preserve thy body and soul unto everlasting life."

Pad looked at the bread.

"Body of ballocks. Eat it yourself." He bit into the cheese.

The chaplain took the bread and ate it, and then cut another piece and gave it wordlessly. Pad swallowed the bread. His face was innocent as a child's.

The chaplain pushed the brandy forward.

"The Blood of our Lord Jesus Christ."

The chaplain was silent.

Pad looked at the bottle, and up again at the chaplain. The chaplain said nothing. Pad laughed, and uncorked the bottle. The chaplain waited. "Slàinte mhaith!" said Pad, tossed back his head and upended the bottle. He gulped several times, set the bottle down and breathed deeply. "Unto everlasting life," said the chaplain, and did the same. He put the cork back.

"Oh," said Pad, "this is the œcumenical time we're having, isn't it, sir? Œcumenical. And that's the big word for a heathen, hedge-school, papist Teigue from Ballimony!" He laughed. "Now it seems it's me mates that have turned in, the idle ones. Would you be keeping me company in this terrible storm with a hand or two of Spoil-Five?"

"Certainly," said the chaplain.

"I'll just get me pack," said Pad, and he winked at William as he felt in his hammock. He sat down again on the table, holding a dismembered book, crudely marked as playing cards. "And would you like to be having a small wager, to give the game an edge, like?"

"How may we wager," said the chaplain, "when we have no spoils in common?"

"Well, sir, how would it be if, every time I lose, that's three Hail Marys, and, if I lose overall, we'll put a Novena on the top of them?"

"And what shall be my wager?" said the chaplain.

"Oh, the pleasure of your company, sir. Indeed, for every game you lose, you shall have a tot of your o-be-joyful; for I'm not the one to make a man sorry over a game of cards."

"You're nothing but a rogue, McAllenan," said the chaplain.

"And aren't all Teigues?" said Pad. "And aren't you the one to know that? But, if you want to put some weight to it, if you lose overall, shall I be taken as your servant, with leave to come and go about the ship while on me duties, and scour no darbies, day or night. How's that for a wager?"

"You would sleep here," said the chaplain.

"But no irons," said Pad.

"No irons," said the chaplain.

"Let me deal you a hand, sir," said Pad. "They're poor things for cards, but a man has to take as he finds."

Pad dealt out the cards, and the chaplain began to pick them up. He stopped.

"This is the Book of Common Prayer!"

"The what, sir? Ah, you've the bee's wisdom on you. But how's an ignorant, heathen, papist, hedge-school Teigue to know it?"

"It is sacrilege!" said the chaplain.

"Could we not say œcumenical, sir, in such a storm as may be the finishing of us? It's a grand sounding word, and no harm meant. Will you not play me œcumenical cards?"

"McAllenan, you're everything I've heard said of you, and more. But, damme, I like your spunk!"

"Well, that's a start," said Pad.

"Then what happens?" said Eggy Mo.

"The giant looks," said William, "and he sees Jack chopping, and he roars and he roars. But Jack chops and he chops; he chops right through that beanstalk."

"Wait on," said Eggy Mo, and was sick again.

"Mr McAllenan can read," Jeremiah whispered.

"How do you know?" said William.

"Watch his eyes."

"The giant swings like a plumbob," said William, holding Eggy Mo's hand again. "What a caterwauling! He tries to get back up the sky; but the more he grabs at the beanstalk, the more it comes away; until, grabbing and tugging, blahting and yowking, he drops right down into the garden, all tangled in the beanstalk."

"The Psalms of David, One and Two," said Jeremiah. "That is the Ace of Spades: or Old Frizzle, as it is known among the Fancy, I believe. And the Ace of Diamonds, the Earl of Cork, is the Table to Find Easter Day."

"And there he lies," said William, "dead as a doornail."

"The Creed of Saint Athanasius is Jack Shepherd, the Knave of Diamonds. I fear that Mr Knopwood is taking too much of the brandy."

"'That's reckoned him up,' says Jack, 'rump and stump, it has. Rump and stump.' And it has. But Jack and his mother, what with the giant's gold, his red hen and the singing harp – well: they're in clover. And, if they're still living, they'll be there yet."

"That was good. I liked that," said Eggy Mo, and he fell out of his hammock into the stew below, and lay there.

"The ten of Hearts is the Table of Kindred and Affinity," said Jeremiah.

They watched.

"Your o-be-joyful's gone, sir. The bottle's empty."

"Lero, lero, lero, lero," said the chaplain.

"So I'll be having the slangs faked tomorrow, sir. And I'll look forward to serving your honour."

Pad gathered the cards. He lifted the chaplain's legs and tucked them about the table's and cradled the bottle in the chaplain's arms. Then he climbed into his hammock.

The ship heeled, and, with only the one dead weight to hold it, the table slid along the deck, drawing the glow of the lantern with it. The chaplain's eyes were closed, but he bounced his buttocks and cried, "Yoiks! Tantivy! Tantivy!"

The Irish turned over to see, awake and grinning.

"Bear a bob, there!" shouted the chaplain as the table reversed and trundled back down the deck. He began to sing.

The Irish took up their spoons and played the tune. The table slid away again, carrying the light, to the furthest reaches of the orlop, but the chaplain's throat was strong.

"There was an old prophesy found in a bog."

"Lilli burlero bullen a-la!" answered the hammocks.

The table disappeared, but for its glow, into the stern, and came back, skidding in the slime.

" 'Ireland shall be ruled by an ass and a dog,' " sang the chaplain.

"Lilli burlero bullen a-la!" echoed the deck.

"Lero lero lilli burlero, lero lero bullen a-la.
"Lero lero lilli burlero, lero lero bullen a-la!"
   The table spun as the ship yawed.
"And now this prophecy is come to pass."
"Lilli burlero bullen a-la!"
"For Talbot's the dog and James is the ass!"
"Lilli burlero bullen a-la!
"Lero lero lilli burlero, lero lero bullen a-la!
"Lero lero lilli burlero, lero lero bullen a-la!!"
   The table upended against the hull, and the chaplain was pitched
into the vomit, his head on Eggy Mo's lap. The lantern went out.
   "Where I dine, I sleep," said the Reverend Robert Knopwood.
   "Amen," said Pad in the dark.

I I

"Well, it's time for me to be breaking Bobby's fast, and get him shaved."

"Would you be so kind, Daniel," said Jeremiah, "as to present Mr Knopwood with my compliments, and to ask him whether he would have the time to spare me a few words?"

"Mother of God! Have you not enough of your own?"

"I wish to speak with him," said Jeremiah.

"Then why didn't you say so?" said Pad.

"He can't help them binnacles," said Renter. "Not like you, putting on the Irish to get Knoppy's red rag out."

"I'm never getting his red rag out," said Pad. "Though he's as fat as a hen in the forehead, still he's a man's man; and I wouldn't flusticate him by being what he thinks I'm not. And if that isn't Irish, what is?"

Pad ran up the companion ladder. In the dusk of the orlop, the silvery twilight that pricked the eyes showed another day had come. The hues were all that told the hours between the far off bells. Groans of dreams, the coughing and gobbing, brought the deck awake. Lines grew for the latrines, and those who would not wait, did not.

"Teddy-me-Godson. Are you in a bate? Oh, you've beshat your hammock, look at you. Come on. Come on. You'll miss your Tommy ration." Renter shook him, paused, and pulled the blanket off, hugging it to himself. "Hey, mates! He's gone to Peg Trantum's!"

There was a rush for the hammock. The body fell to the deck, and men seized on it, fighting over the carrion. Only the trousers were left, and that only because the irons snagged them.

"Put him back," said Renter, when there was nothing else to be had. "And cover him in tidy."

"It's good," said Renter, holding the blanket to the light. "In the nick."

"How may you?" said Jeremiah.

"When mine's rags? This'll dry."

"I've got a shoe," said Eggy Mo.

"One shoe?" said Jeremiah.

"Ay."

"Does it fit?" said William.

"Nearly," said Eggy Mo.

"You're a grand un," said William.

"Good-day to you, Mr Erbin."

The chaplain came down the companion ladder, followed by Pad.

"Good-day, Mr Knopwood."

"And a fine day it is, too," said the chaplain. "All in all, we have had a fair voyage, since Rio and the Cape. Last night, I took my pipe on deck, and looked up at the sky clifted with stars; and such stars, sir! Though, to see Orion invert brings thoughts of what a mighty feat, with God's help, His Majesty's oak and canvas may achieve at the hand of man. But such stars!"

"Ah, there, perforce, you have the advantage of us," said Jeremiah.

"Forgive me," said the chaplain. "In the drawing of attention to your situation, I was most remiss."

"To draw your attention was the burden of my request," said Jeremiah.

"And what may that be?" said the chaplain.

"The heat in these latitudes," said Jeremiah. "The heat, sir; the temper and very quiddity of the air; the faecal ejecta; the urinary graveolence; the gynaecian catamenia; our sudorous foedity – "

"He means we stink, sir," said Pad.

"Can nothing be done that a soul may breathe? Why, but this very morning – "

"Stubble it!" whispered Renter.

"I shall speak with the surgeon," said the chaplain. "I believe that the burning of sea coals is most efficacious in these matters, and does purify the noxious elements. And, to that end, I bid you once more good-day."

He went back up the companion ladder, with Pad in attendance.

"Why did you silence me?" Jeremiah said to Renter.

"All on account of you were a-going to blow the gab on Teddy-me-Godson," said Renter.

"But the man is dead, and requires committal."

"Not yet, he don't," said Renter. "There's eight days' victuals to be drawn against his name before he comes so hogo we can't ride the strength of him."

12

"Why are you set on it?" said William.

The men were clearing a space along the orlop. They pushed the chairs and tables against the hull, and lashed the hammocks, except for the stained one that hung above its wetness on the deck floor.

"Your companions have invited you to be of their inner circle of acquaintance," said Jeremiah. "It would be discourteous, and folly, to refuse."

"But what's the odds, when I'm going home?"

"But if you are not?"

"But I am. And Pad. And Eggy Mo. And Renter. And it's Renter as is the governor of this lot. So why?"

"Ah, friend Charles," said Jeremiah. "I agree: Charles is of a devious nature, and one for any sport."

"Come with us."

"I fear that the geography would test not only my intellect but my constitution, William. But my heart will dwell on you, as I labour under a southern sun."

"You think I shan't do it, don't you?"

"Not so much 'will not' as 'cannot'," said Jeremiah. "I look at you, and the picture is ever before my eyes:

'O nimium caelo et pelago confise sereno,

Nudus in ignota, Palinure, iacebis harena.' "

William frowned, and worked his lips. " 'Sky and sea . . . Happy in the sand with nowt too much on his ignorant cufuffle'? No.

That's reckoned me up."

" 'O Palinurus, too trusting in heaven and a calm sea, you shall lie naked on an unknown sand.' " said Jeremiah.

"Who's Pallywhatsit?"

"A man who thought that he knew whither he was going, and took no heed."

"Yay, but he didn't have this, did he?" said William, and reached into his pocket. He opened his fist carefully. The quartz was dull in the grey light; yet, deep down, was the shadow of a rainbow.

"And what may that be?" said Jeremiah.

"Me swaddledidaff."

"And that is what?"

"A promise," said William. "My promise. Don't you let on."

Jeremiah looked at William.

"Ay," he said. "I would trust that where I would not your compass."

William nodded, and put the swaddledidaff back in his pocket. "Port Jackson. China. Turn left. And straight home."

"Yet you are not troubled at the thought of our sable brethren, the Indians?"

"Oh, they're nowt, by all accounts; what there is of them."

"They are cannibal. Fee, fi, fo, fum, William. Fee, fi, fo. And the fum."

"Are you there?" called Renter. "It's time!"

"I'm coming!" said William.

"Nil desperandum," said Jeremiah.

"It's daft," said William.

Renter was sitting on a table in the middle of the deck. William went and stood before him.

"Are you ready and desirous to be Stalled to the Rogue?" said Renter.

"I am," said William.

"And are you ready and desirous to take the Oath, and, with it, a new name?"

"I am," said William.

"Then swear on Man Thomas and on bawbles."

William drew a deep breath, closed his eyes and spoke at a gallop of concentration.

"I do swear on Man Thomas and on bawbles that I, Crank Cuffin, shall be a true brother, and that I will obey the commands of the great tawny prince, and keep his counsel.

"I will take my prince's part against all that do oppose him; nor will I suffer him, or any one belonging to us, to be abused by any strange abrams, rufflers, hookers, pailliards, swaddlers, Irish toyles – "

"Oh, they're the ones!" shouted Pad.

"Shurrup. I'll forget. Irish toyles, swigmen, whip jacks, jarkmen, bawdy baskets, dommerars, clapperdodgeons, patricoes or curtals.

"I will not conceal aught I win out of libkins or from the ruffmans.

"Lastly, I will cleave to my doxy wap stiffly, and will bring her duds, marjery praters, gobblers, grunting cheats or tibs of the buttery, is winnings for her weppings."

A cheer broke out, and voices called: "Well told, Crank!" "Very good tale!" Renter lifted up a tin mug of lime juice and vinegar, and poured it over William's head, and shouted for all to hear: "I, dimber-damber and upright-man, with this gage of bowse, do Stall thee, Crank Cuffin, to the Rogue! And from henceforth it shall be lawful for thee to cant for thy living in all places!"

There was more cheering, and Renter got down from the table and stood, facing William. Then a rhythm of leg irons being clinked together built up. Others joined, to a different beat. And the deeper notes of the long chains were added. William and Renter began to dance around each other, with as much grace as their own irons would allow. Pad and the Irish started to sing, and all joined in.

> "Bing out, bien morts, and toure and toure,
> Bing out, bien morts, and toure;
> For all your duds are binged awast;
> The bien cove hath the loure,
> The loure,
> The bien cove hath the loure!"

Another cheer, and Pad called, "You now, Crank! Let's have one from you! And let's have it a dance for us!"

"I can't," said William. "I'm no singer."

"Oh, but you are!" said Pad. "There's devil a man without a song!"

"Well," said William, "I've a little ditty as we had used to sing at home every year."

"And is there a dance in it?"

"Ay – there is."

"Come on, then! Bear a bob!"

The chains began to ring in waiting: clink, clink, clink, clink.

"Faster," said William. "Same as this: Di-dee, di-dee, di-diddle-di-dee." They picked up the tune, and William sang.

> "I'll dye, I'll dye my petticoat red;
> For the lad I love I'd bake my bread;
> And then my daddy would wish that I were dead;
> Sweet Willy in the morning among the rush!"

Already the men and women were dancing, and the sound of their chains hammered through the deck.

"Together now!" said William.

> "Shoorly, shoorly, shoo-gang-rowl!
> Shoo-gang-lolly-mog, shoog-a-gang-a-low!
> Sweet Willy in the morning among the rush!"

"Oh, that's the fine tune!" cried Pad. "Let's be having it again, and every Jack-rag of you singing!"

The noise was tremendous. The whole ship resounded to voice and iron.

Jeremiah watched.

"It would seem that the sea coals did their work," said the chaplain. He had come down unnoticed in the tumult.

"As may be," said Jeremiah. "For myself, I must own that they but piled Pelion on Ossa with their smoke. Though it may be said that the admixture did confound the individualities."

The second round of the dance ended.

"Is there room for another at the horky?" shouted the chaplain.

"Come down, sir!" said Pad. "But you must sing your dues!"

"Sing?" said the chaplain. "I'll dance 'em! And you'll be chorus! Are you ready now for 'The Merry Golden Tree'?"

"Aye aye!" came the answer, with rattling chains.

"Make space, then! For I've some spring to me!"

The crowd parted, the chaplain struck a pose, leapt and began:

"There was a gallant ship, and a gallant ship was she!"

"Eck iddle du, and the Lowlands low!" howled the chorus.

"And she was called 'The Merry Golden Tree'!"

"As she sailed to the Lowlands low!"

The chaplain bounded across the deck.

"She had not sailed a league, a league but only three!"

"Eck iddle du, and the Lowlands low!"

"When she came up with a French gallee!"

"As she sailed to the Lowlands low!"

The chaplain made a pirouette, and clicked his heels.

"Out spoke the little cabin-boy, out spoke he!"

"Mother of God. The hammock."

"Eck iddle du, and the Lowlands low!"

"'What will you give me if I sink that French gallee?'!"

"'As ye sail to the Lowland – '"

The chaplain stepped in the puddle of moisture, slipped, and fell across the slung hammock, face down.

"Oh, Christ and His Saints."

There was not a breath, not a chink.

"This man," said the chaplain. "How long has he been dead?"

"Dead, sir." said Pad.

"He is putrefaction."

"Well, we did think he was in a bit of a sulk."

"Sulk?"

"But then he was never the great talker."

"And you claim to have smelt nothing."

"We thought it was the fumigatising you did, sir."

The chaplain stood and lapped the edges of the hammock over and made the sign of the cross above it. He walked along the deck, and the crowd opened for him in silence. At the companion ladder he turned, and said, "I shall send those to sew him in. Four of you to carry." And he left.

No one spoke. No one moved. Two sailors, and armed guard, came down; and they sewed the hammock into a shroud with twine. They laid the leg chain along the body.

"Take 'em off him!" said William. "Don't send him in slangs!"

"He needs the weight," said Jeremiah.

"He must go down free!"

"He is free," said Jeremiah.

The sailors finished the job, and went. Pad lifted the body onto his shoulder and made for the companion. He moved his head. "Who's for some air?"

Renter took the lashings of one end and gave a handful to Eggy Mo. William and Jeremiah took the other end.

"Follow me," said Pad. "And easy does it."

The body was nothing, but their irons made them unsteady on

the ladder.

"Watch for your eyes up top," said Pad. "It's a honeycomb of ages since you've seen such light."

They went on the companion through the decks and out at the top. They yelled, and dropped the body, covering their faces with their hands.

"Didn't I tell you?" said Pad, himself squinting.

They parted their fingers. The light was agony, and there was no colour but yellow gold. Gold deck. Gold mast. Gold sail. Gold agony of sky. Gold agony of flashing sea. No depth. No shade. All gold.

"Take him up," said the voice of the chaplain, "and bear him here."

There were the shapes of golden men, outlined in a greater gold, standing at a gold bulwark.

"Here's me hand," said Pad, gripping William's. They lifted the body again, and Pad led them along the deck.

There was a plank already balanced on the after-rail, steadied by marines. Next to it were the Captain, the surgeon and the chaplain.

"Lay him on the plank," said the chaplain. "Take hold." The marines stepped back. William, Jeremiah, Renter and Eggy Mo held the plank.

"He did ought to go down free," said William.

"The sea-lawyers will look to that," said Pad, "when they render their account."

Colour was coming back into the air, and William could open his eyes. He saw the water behind the ship slit by fins.

"Have you command of yourselves, Erbin?" said the chaplain.

"We have, sir," said Jeremiah.

"Commit the body when I signify."

"We shall, sir."

The water was flecked with blue.

The chaplain opened his book.

" 'I am the resurrection and the life, saith the Lord; he that believeth in me, though he were dead, yet shall he live; and whosoever liveth and believeth in me shall never die – ' "

"Oh, fake the slangs," William sobbed.

" 'Man that is born of woman hath but a short time to live, and is full of misery – ' "

Take them off!

" 'In the midst of life we are in death – ' "

Off! Off! Off!

" ' – suffer us not, in our last hour, for any pains of death, to fall from thee.'

"What may we say of our brother, Christopher, here departed?"

"Non omnis moriar," said Jeremiah.

"He was sore afflicted; yet, in his affliction, we may see eternal hope still shine, and say with him: Yea! He did chase them. His apron he did flap at them. But they did see him coming. They did see his apron. Yet shall he get them. One day."

" 'I shall not entirely die,' " Jeremiah said to William.

The chaplain nodded, and Jeremiah lifted the end of the plank. The hammock slid, and dropped.

"We therefore commit this body to the deep, to be turned into corruption, looking for the resurrection of the body, when the Sea shall give up her dead, and the life of the world to come – "

"He's not sinking," said Eggy Mo.

"Too much gas in him," said Renter.

The shroud bobbed in the water, and slowly went under.

"Land ho!" cried the look-out from the crow's nest.

"Na-a-a-a-y!" shouted William. "But you could have waited! Why did you not wait on? And lay him in earthen lake?"

"Land ho!"

" – who at His coming shall change our vile body, that it may be like His glorious body – "

"The sea-lawyers would appear to contest the brief," said Jeremiah.

13

William was as far forward as he could get in the boat. He could smell and taste the earth on the air. The colours of green to the edge of blue, and broken by the trunks of silver trees. The tents and stores of the landing party, the fires on the beach, and the chaplain's marquee were separated from this world by the line of the perimeter guard; but which side was the guarded, William could not see.

He jumped the instant he felt the keel grate. He disappeared, but rose again to his waist and began to labour for the shore. He swung from side to side with his chains; then he was in foam, and his step reached land. Though it heaved under him in its stillness, he kept himself firm.

"I'm coming. Not long now, Het. I'm here."

The others were behind him in the water. Some had to be pulled up from drowning. Some moved as though drunk. Some crawled onto the sand. Some lay, too dizzy to move, until kicked to their legs.

Men went down from the camp and waded out to unload the boat. The new men were formed up to have their chains unlocked. William stood in his chains, and felt them, one by one, taken from him.

I've bested you. You bugger.

Yet they still held him. He had to force his arms apart, and there was no weight to them. He took a step, but could not raise his foot from a shuffle.

He made himself lift, and the leg that had worn the long chain, now without its heaviness, jerked upwards and out, and he fell. On hands and knees, he tried to stand, but he had no balance without iron, and fell again.

"Easy does it, Crank," said Pad, and kept him steady while he teetered upright. "You'll soon be in fine twig. Just keep on the go till you find yourself."

"Get. Me. Home."

William walked. The heavy chain leg strode too far each time, so that his knees bent at a square angle and he sank at his hips. Pad gripped his upper arm and elbow and forced him along the beach. They turned back at the guard line, and walked again. His legs straightened and the rise and dip of his head grew less, until Pad could let go of the arm, and William's stagger became a slow, but even, pace. They came to a fire. "Good as caz," said Pad. "He'll be good as caz."

Renter and Jeremiah were sitting by the smouldering wood, and Eggy Mo was waddling up and down, without his leg irons, trying to stride, but he, too, was thrown by the missing long chain.

"Welcome to New Holland," said Jeremiah; "or to that part of it that is now Sullivan Bay, for such has been its nomenclature for the past week. It strikes me as remarkable how those in authority seem to be unable to recognise a place until they have named it, though there can be no doubt of its existence before our coming.

"Now. Take meat and drink, William; but I suggest that you remain standing until you are in full command of your limbs, for I consider it essential, since you are determined on your leaving, that you do not delay, but go while there is still some disorder in the camp. To which end, always be sure to carry something and to move as with purpose, then no one will distract you from your true errand of seeking provender. Why have you not yet been issued with clothing?"

"There was none as would fit," said William. "The quarter-master says it'll have to be made special."

"Then you must go as you are," said Jeremiah. "And you may be the better for it. The new cloth does scoriate the tender parts most grievously, and hampers movement."

"But it doesn't eat the night out of you," said Pad. "And we're well rid of our old togs, eh?" He laughed with Renter.

"It was the best Adam Tilering I've seen in a long while," said Renter, and pointed to Jeremiah. "Don't let them binnacle words fool you. That one could make his fortune."

"I'm fit," said William. "Let's be off."

"Wait while I tell you, won't you?" said Pad. "Oh, it was beautiful. It was gorgeous. You see, Bobby isn't the one to live in a tent. Oh no. There's no room for his dining table. So he ships out his own marquee, and there's no rest for us till it's up and to his liking. Then there's himself, standing over his goods and chattels on the shore, and me toing and froing with his comestibles, as he calls them. Now there's a word."

"Are you with me, or aren't you?"

"Festina lente, William," said Jeremiah. "All in its season."

"Eh! I'm walking proper!" said Eggy Mo.

"So I takes four bottles of his liquid comestibles, and wraps them in a bit of old sacking; and there's meself out of the marquee with it, past the guard, when who goes by but this old reprobate, with a sack of his own, not looking, and knocks right into me. 'Arrah,' says I, 'do you squint like a bag of nails, that you can't see a man before you?' "

"And I says, 'Hold your mag, frig pig,' " said Renter, " 'or your glims'll be shining like a shitten door.' "

"Frig pig, he calls me! 'Who, you, you moving dunghill?' says I. 'You piss more than you drink!' Well, the guard knows trouble's on the way, so he's quick to send us packing, and on I goes with me little bundle."

"And I'm shouting, 'I'll mill your glaze for you!', said Renter, "when round the corner of the marquee, slap bang, this one steps;

and he's got his bundle, too."

"I can run! I can run!" cried Eggy Mo.

"Anyway," said Renter, "out come the binnacle words. 'Oh, Charles!' he says. 'Charles! My sincere apologies!' he says. 'I was the cause entirely!', or some such. And he starts turning me round, and making me tidy; and I shove him off, and he goes one way, and I goes t'other."

"I can't eat any more," said William.

"Put it in your shirt, and take my drinking can, and do not part with it," said Jeremiah.

"And there's me, down the beach with Bobby," said Pad, "and him standing over his furniture like it was a saint's bones."

"But these britches is giving me jockam some gee up," said Eggy Mo.

"So do it in your hands and rub it in," said Renter.

" 'Oh,' " says Bobby, 'what's that you're carrying, McAllenan, from my marquee?' "

" 'Oh,' " says I, " 'it's me old togs, sir, for the fire. There's no wear left in them, and besides, they're walking. Indeed, I don't know why I carry the idle creatures.' And I throws the bundle on the fire, and up it goes in flames, with the creatures crackling in it. 'Well,' I says, 'I promised them hell fire, and now they're there straight, and no purgatory.' "

"Choice," said Renter. "Very choice."

"The long and the short of it, William," said Jeremiah, "is that, having ascertained which of the marines can least hold their liquor, I have persuaded them, by letting them see what is in my gift, that they should stand guard together this evening on the eastern perimeter, where I shall visit them an hour or so before sunset. And you and your companions shall happen to pass that way in the gloaming, when we shall see whether yet again the peculiar ability of the Irish to wage war with brandy wine has been successful."

"Ah, it's only four bottles of red tape I could get," said Pad. "With two of me granny's poteen, they'd not see a hole in a ladder."

14

The air was purple; the sky; the sea; the sand; the grass; the trees; all purple.

"Well, lads, shall us be doing?" said William.

"Aye aye, Crank!" said Eggy Mo.

"And think on: no stopping; and no rush. See you, there's Jeremiah."

"He's done his job, by the looks of things," said Renter.

"Ah, but that red tape: it's not the stuff to make the likes of them paralyticised. I'm not easy," said Pad.

"Right," said William. "Come on."

They began to walk towards where Jeremiah was with four of the guard, who were leaning on their flintlocks more as props than guns.

William, Eggy Mo, Renter and Pad carried tin mugs, and bread and meat wrapped in sacking.

"Now be listening to me," said William, "and take no notice of them, same as they weren't there."

Other food was in their clothing, which fitted so badly that they looked no more misshapen than any of the rest.

"Once upon a time ago," said William, "Henny-Penny were in the stackyard."

"It was the field," said Renter.

"It were the stackyard. It had to be the stackyard, didn't it, because that's where the oak were, else it couldn't have happened, could it?"

"No, it couldn't've," said Eggy Mo. "Go on, Crank."

"There she is in the stackyard," said William, "when, thump, wallop, down comes an acorn and hits her on the head."

"Does it hurt?" said Eggy Mo.

"Not a lot," said William, "but, 'Eh up!' says Henny-Penny. 'The sky's a-going to fall. I must tell king.' "

"Why?" said Renter.

"Never you mind," said William. "It's got nowt to do with you."

The guard looked up. Jeremiah laughed, and passed round a bottle.

"So she goes along and she goes along and she goes along, until who should she meet but Cocky-Locky. 'Where are you going, Henny-Penny?' says Cocky-Locky."

" 'I'm going to tell king the sky's a-falling,' says Henny-Penny. 'Oh, I'll come with you,' says Cocky-Locky. So Henny-Penny and Cocky-Locky go to tell king the sky's a-falling."

"And was it?" said Eggy Mo.

"They thought as it were, and that's all what matters," said William. "Anyroad, they goes along and they goes along and they goes along, when who should they meet but Ducky-Daddles."

"I think it was just an acorn," said Eggy Mo.

"Oh, thee hold thy rattle," said William. "And Ducky-Daddles says, 'Where are you going, Henny-Penny and Cocky-Locky?' "

"Wasn't it Foxy-Woxy?" said Renter.

"No it weren't," said William. "That's later. And you be told, and all."

"Eh. And where do you think you're off to?" said one of the guard. "Halt. Who goes there? Friend or foe?"

"Friend. We're going to tell king the sky's a-falling," said William.

"Advance, friend, and be recognised," said the guard. "Parole."

" 'Sullivan'," said William. "And Counter Sign, 'Woodriff'."

"Pass, friend," said the guard.

"Foxy-Woxy," said another marine. "Foxy-Woxy. Poxy-Doxy." He giggled. "Doxy-poxy-woxy-foxy. Poxy-foxy-woxy-doxy."

They stepped over the boundary of the camp.

"And the fum, William," said Jeremiah in a whisper. "The fum!"

" 'Then I'll come with you,' says Ducky-Daddles." Their backs were now to the guard.

"Ah well, Bobby got his Parole right, and that's a mercy," said Pad.

"So Ducky-Daddles, Cocky-Locky and Henny-Penny go to tell king the sky's a-falling."

"Ain't the king in London?" said a marine.

"You're right! He is! Oi! You! Come back here!"

"Take no notice. 'So they goes along and they goes along and they goes along, when who should they meet but Goosey-Poosey – ' "

"Halt!"

"Don't run. 'Where are you going, Henny-Penny, Cocky-Locky and Ducky-Daddles?' says Goosey-Poosey."

"Halt! Or I fire!"

" 'We're going to tell king the sky's a-falling.' "

There was a crack, and a ball ripped past them.

"Nedash, Crank!" Eggy Mo stopped. "The caterpillars are down!" He turned, and put his hands above his head. "I give up! Don't shoot!" The guard fired again. Eggy Mo ran towards the camp. "I give up! Mam!" There was another shot, and Eggy Mo dropped.

"Cut stick!" shouted Pad, and the three scattered.

The lieutenant and more marines came running, pushed the staggering guard aside and took aim.

"Wait!" called the chaplain. He was hurrying from his marquee.

"I cannot wait, sir!" said the lieutenant. "There has been a breakout!"

"Give the hare law," said the chaplain. "McAllenan! Come back, you fool! McAllenan! There's nowhere for you! Come back!"

"In your own time!" ordered the lieutenant. "Free fire!"

Pad sprawled on his stomach. William swerved to him.

"Cut stick, Crank. I'm bung upward, me."

"Give us your arm!"

"We're spoiled and boned. The compass. Me pocket."

William crouched as the air tore. He dragged a sheet of crumpled paper from the pocket.

"This?"

But Pad was fingering small stones from the beach, passing them through his hand. "Ave Maria gratia plena Dominus tecum benedicta tu in mulieribus et benedictus fructus ventris tui ave Maria gratia plena Dominus tecum benedicta tu in mulieribus et benedictus fructus ventris tui ave Maria gratia plena Dominus tecum benedicta tu in mulieribus et benedictus fructus ventris tui ave Maria gratia plena Dominus tecum benedicta tu in mulieribus et benedictus fructus ventris tui ave Maria gratia plena Dominus tecum – "

William ran. He could not run straight, but his mind would not let his legs fail.

"Crank!"

Renter was lying on the sand.

"Haul your wind, Crank."

"Gerrup!"

"It's all holiday in Peckham, Crank."

William put his hand in Renter's wet shirt to take the food. He grappled with the body to make it sit. "Damn you! Gerrup!" The meat slid away from him around the back. He put both arms in, and pushed one way and pulled the other, to bring it round to the front. And all the time he crouched against the tearing. "Dall yer eyes!" But he had hold of a bone, and tugged the meat out and ran.

"Cease firing!"

The lieutenant waved his hand at the dusk.

"Save your powder. He'll be back, or come never."

Jeremiah watched the purple shadow merge.

" 'The bright day is done. And we are for the dark.' I fear me, Mr Johnson."

III

YOUNG COB

Mony klyf he ouerclambe in contrayez straunge,
Fer floten fro his frendez fremedly he rydez.

"Sir Gawain and the Green Knight"
lines 713/4

15

He ran under the moon. The moon set. He ran under the stars. The stars paled. He ran along the surf, leaving no trace. He ran as fast as a man could walk. He ran bent double, as he had stood in the months below decks, knowing no other, his hands scuffing the water. His legs wavered, his right foot stepping across to the left, his left to the right. He ran into the green of the rising sun. William ran.

He stopped, and listened. There was only the great silence of the waves. He hutched himself round to face the way he had come. It was easier to move in the water, because it gave his legs the weight of the chain and the irons. He tilted his head sideways to look. The mast of the ship was on the horizon, and blue smoke from the camp rose in the air, but the shore and the land were empty: sand, grass, low trees here and there, silver, brown, green. But nobody; no pursuit or chase. He grunted.

Now then.

It took five moves to turn back. He tilted his head again. The shore curved away, and hills near to.

Compass.

He smoothed the crumpled paper.

What the heck?

There was a circle drawn on the paper, quartered by a cross. At the top of one arm was the letter N and an arrow.

N? N?

He tilted his head all around, but he saw no N.

What's N? And the arrow? Is it pointing? N pointing?

Fause monkey! Port Jackson! China! It's North!

William held the paper so that the arrow pointed away from him along the shore. He held it steady, and walked forward.

Eh up, Het!

16

It was worse than the bread of that day: the burnt bread with God's blessing. It was the white bread with God's curse. He had snapped off a crust and put it in his mouth and sat under a tree out of the sun.

The bread was bone. There was nothing in his mouth to soften it. His tongue stuck to the lump. He moved it around. Bone. He granched it with his teeth, and tried to swallow, but his throat would not. He chewed the lump to splinter, the splinter to shard, the shard to crumb, and spat, but he could not rid his mouth. He had to scrape out the dust with his fingers.

The sun had moved, and he shifted away.

He took a piece of beef, but the brine was too harsh. He pulled at grass, cutting his hands, and pushed it into his mouth. It changed the taste, but gave him no juice. He gagged on the dryness and heaved it from him. He turned his palms, and, with slow care, picked each bead of blood on his tongue. It was salt, but he could feel the moist for an instant as it was taken up. He sat against the trunk and closed his eyes.

The sun hurt his lids. It had moved again. He looked at the shadow, and at where he had first sat. There was only the air beating down. Where he had shifted, too, was in the open light.

Yay! Bugger this for a game! Sun's going backards!

Skrike or laugh, said Grandad. You'll learn.

He collapsed against the tree. A wind blew from the land; and on it was a sweet and biting scent. He sniffed. It was the smell in the sound of the bee at the churching.

Gripe, griffin, hold fast!

William kept the compass straight, and ran in the sun, along the shore, laughing, though his skin cracked.

17

Well, this won't buy the child a new frock.

He drank from the river as much as he could, took the bread from the pool where it had been soaking, and ate half of it. He dipped the tin mug into the water and filled it, then he stood, straightened his back, and set off along the shore, slowly, carefully, trying not to slop from the mug, which he held in one hand, the compass in the other, following N.

There was no shade from the sun, and, as it rose higher, the compass pointed towards it.

Ay, you would! Get on, then, chase-yer-arse! See if I'm frit!

The water and the sky became one light, and the bread began to harden in his shirt. He sucked the bread until there was no more to be got from it. His head ached. He put the bread by a tussock, and the mug with it, holding down the compass, and went into the sea. He sat, and dipped his head in the waves. The water burnt his face, but it cooled him. He looked around. There was only the shore, backed by hills, stretching in front and behind, so that, without the compass, both ways would have been the same. The river was lost, and there was no sign of any other.

When the sun was lowering, he came out of the water and went back to the tussock. The mug and the compass were as he had left them, but the bread had gone.

What the ferrips?

There were crumbs in the sand. Some were moving.

He looked closely. The crumbs were being carried by ants.

They've getten me pannam!

He picked up the crumbs that were lying and ate each one as if it were a meal. He felt a stab of fire at his foot. An ant had taken hold of his flesh. He knocked it away, and the body snapped off, leaving the head still in him.

Best be doing, said Grandad.

William took up the mug and the compass, checked the N, and moved forward.

He was thirsty. He sipped at the water. It was not enough. He dipped a piece of meat into the mug, and sucked that. But the brine was stronger than the water, and his thirst grew. His ankle throbbed and was swelling. To drink was all his head could hold. But he would not.

The sun dried his clothes, and they stiffened with the salt. The seams rubbed him so that he cried out. His hand shook, and water splashed over the rim. He knelt and tried to save the spillage, but the sand had taken it. He drank. He could not stop. He could not stop. He tilted the mug and stretched for more, but he touched nothing but metal.

William looked along the N into the fret of sea and light and land. Nothing.

Nowt.

Best be doing, then, said Grandad.

William cast around with his head. The sun hurt as much as his ankle.

Nothing.

He turned, and set off back the way he had come. He could hobble.

He fell into the river in the purple light. He put his head under the clear stream until he had no breath. Then he pulled himself out and lay by the bank, and chewed some meat.

Well, this won't buy the child a new frock.

He had lain in the shade by the river and cooled his leg in the water until the swelling had gone. There was no more bread, and only enough meat to last him to China, but he reckoned the folks there wouldn't let him starve, for all they were blue. He filled his mug with water.

He followed his footprints in the sand, past where he had sat in the sea, a half day more, but the meat made him drink, and he got back to the river because the grass had become dewed in the night.

Well, this won't buy the child a new frock.

He filled his mug, and set off in the dark, not drinking, but licking the grass until day, and all that day he did not eat, but the mug was emptied and he had reached no water. On the way back, another night came, and he tried not to eat, but had to, and he coughed and spewed, but he found the river before dawn, and was safe.

Well, this won't buy the child a new frock.

He watched two whole moons go round before he felt strong enough to leave the river, and even so he had to turn back to it again, while he could.

Well, this won't buy the child a new frock.

He came to new water. It was a stream that he must have nearly reached before, but he had always stopped too soon. He dipped his head and gulped. The water was salt, scalding his face and shrivelling his throat. He did not remember how he got back to the river.

He practised. He made himself do with less and less water, until he could go for three days without putting the mug in the river. But he knew that did not mean there would be another river, however many days he walked.

Well, this won't buy the child a new frock.

There was no more meat. He could fill his mug, and he could stand. All night and all day he walked. His feet had lost feeling, and his hands tingled, and there was no sweat for him to breathe; but the mug was full. He licked dew the next night also, and spilled never a drop of the water. He passed the salt stream, which told him he could not go back, but N was steady and William in fine twig. The sun rose behind him into a new day.

"Bear a bob!" he cried. And Niggy Bower and John Stayley, and Joshua and Charlie, Sam, Isaac and Elijah began to sing with William.

> " 'Who would true valour see
>> Let him come hither!
> One here will constant be,
>> Come wind, come weather!' "

William turned, and walked backwards, but holding the compass straight, and the mug steady. They were all marching after, led by Tiddy Turnock and Squarker Kennerley, in uniform and holding their staffs and singing.

> " 'There's no discouragement
> Shall make him once relent
> His first avowed intent
> To be a pilgrim!' "

The church band was at the rear: Bongy Blackshaw played the serpent; Mazzer Massey the violin; Juggy Potts the clarinet. And, out on a rock in the sea, Cobby Lawton sat with his bass viol.

> " 'Whoso beset him round
>> With dismal stories,
> Do but themselves confound;
>> His strength the more is!' "

William faced the front, beating time with the compass hand.

> " 'No lion can him fright;
> He'll with a giant fight,
> But he will have the right
>> To be a pilgrim!'

[108]

"Eh!" said William. "Where's wenches? Where's Het?"

Tiddy and Squarker smiled.

This here's lads' stuff, youth.

> 'Hobgoblin nor foul fiend
>> Can daunt his spirit!
> He knows he at the end
>> Shall life inherit!
> Then, fancies, flee away;
> He'll not fear what men say;
> He'll labour night and day
>> To be a pilgrim!'

By, but it's dusty work, this ranting! Give us a sup!

And they crowded round him, Cobby wading from his rock, and took the mug, and all drank their fill.

"Nay! You munner!" shouted William.

Cobby winked at him, and sang:

> 'Owd Cob and Young Cob
> And Young Cob's son;
> Young Cob's Owd Cob
> When Owd Cob's done!'

He drank.

"You munner!"

Cobby gave the mug back to William, and the band turned and marched away, following Tiddy and Squarker, playing and singing.

> 'Owd Cob and Young Cob
> And Young Cob's son!
> Young Cob's Owd Cob
> When Owd Cob's done!'

"You munner."

The beach was empty. The mug was dry.

But there was a bead. One bead of water on the tin.

William tipped the mug, and the bead slid to the bottom. He carried it as gently as if the mug were full. The compass and the bead. They were everything through that day. In the bead he sometimes found a rainbow, small, but a rainbow the same as at the mere, as in the swaddledidaff that wore his pocket thin.

It caught the first of the evening. And William did not see the rock, and stumbled, one shoe splitting as he fell, and he lay, watching the bead trickle out onto the rock. It rolled to the stem of a blue flower that grew in a crack, a flower that he had known somewhere, and soaked down to the root.

William heard a humming, and smelt the sweet sharp air of the church and the wind off the land. A bee, small as a fly, hovered on the petal, and lifted nectar from the flower's heart.

"Fair do's," said William. "Ay. Fair do's, and all."

18

The bee's wings brought him out of blackness. He did not want them to. They came, and went, came, and went, but they would not go. Soon, they were louder, and he could not stay asleep. He opened his eyes.

It was daylight, but dark. He was lying in the sand. It was not the bee; it was thunder banging on the mountains: two peaks standing alone, and lightning about them.

Splashes of rain hit his face, and the splashes turned to a pouring, and he opened his mouth and drank the water that the bee thunder gave back to him from the root of the blue flower and the nectar of its heart.

> Oh, can you wash a soldier's shirt?
> And can you wash it clean?
> Oh, can you wash a soldier's shirt,
> And hang it on the green?

He danced, but his broken shoe made him stamp. Under the rain he stamped. He stamped his keggly shoe from him.

> Oh, can you wash a soldier's shirt?
> And can you wash it clean?
> Oh, can you wash a soldier's shirt,
> And hang it on the green?

He took the shoe soles and clapped to the tread of a foot that now knew land.

"And I can wash a soldier's shirt! And I can wash it clean! And I can wash a soldier's shirt, and hang it on the green!"

The sun set behind him. Another moon rose in front. The rain had filled his mug, but he had long finished it. And the rivers and streams were all salt now: rivers and streams of flowing salt into the sea; and there was marsh. Even the dew tasted of it.

Never mind, Het.

He could follow the compass in the light. Towards dawn, he saw a rock ahead, going down to the tide. He would find snails there. The sky was bright behind the rock when he got to it, and he put the compass under the mug, and walked into the sea, feeling for the shells. The flesh was tough, but in each was a squirt of clean water, and he swallowed without chewing, once he had burst the gut. He ate as much as he could. Each bite was a step to China; his belly was his baggin cloth. As long as there was baggin, he was right for another day, and he made the juice of the snails taste of cold tea.

He went back for the mug and the compass. N pointed over the rock, and he climbed up to follow it.

"Barley mey!"

Below the rock, the shore ran to a point. The sea was on both sides. Across the water, the shore began again, and there the ship was at anchor. Along the beach smoke rose from the camp, which was now ordered rows of tents and huts; and gardens. And Knoppy's marquee. There was a pole. From it hung the Union Jack. He saw marines at drill in squares. There were sailors. Jeremiah waved to him.

He looked at the compass. N pointed at them. But the paper was torn, the folds cracked. It was coming to pieces in his hands.

"Tha's bugger't; and tha's bugger't me," said William.

He looked again over the water.

He could smell the comfort of a fire in the night, and new baked bread, and he could smell fresh water, and there were bright colours, and friends that would talk outside his head. And there were buildings painted white, with no windows and one door and heavy bolts; and men working in lines, and straight lines, and straight fences, and straight paths and straight roads: prison bars reaching out to gridiron the shore and hill, not seeing how the land danced.

Falseness and guile, said Tiddy, have reigned too long.

And truth, said Squarker, hath been set under a lock.

"No back bargains!" shouted William, turned and jumped.

At the even, said Tiddy, men heareth the day.

To get from the sea, William fled by left and right, among tussocks and dunes, through mud pools, he kicked his one shoe away. He followed a stream against its flow. Even here, when sun and moon were mad, and N came round, streams, even salt, would not start at the sea.

He was among low hills and trees when he fell. He could not stand. The last thing he saw was the arrow, pointing away from where he had come.

"Tha's still bugger't."

He must have been lying too long. The sun was burning him sick through the shade of the few trees. The ground was brittle leaves and twigs and bark, a bed of tinder. The mug and the compass were in front of him. He looked at the compass, then at the tinder. It hurt his head to move, and his tongue was swollen so that he had to breathe through his nose. His fingers twitched in the litter, picking bits over. He found a piece of bark as soft as linen. He spread it under his palm, next to the compass.

He felt for a strong twig, and took it between his fingers. He tested along his arm for a boil that was ripe, and probed and pressed it with the twig until the boil broke. He squeezed out the pus down to the blood, and, when the liquor was red, he began to copy the pattern of the compass onto the bark, using the twig as a brush: first, the circle and the cross; next the arrow, taking care that it was pointing as the arrow on the paper; and, at the top, a new N.

She'll do.

He held the bark compass, gripped the mug, and pushed himself to his knees. He crawled to a tree, and hugged his body upright against the trunk. He inched until his back was against the tree, and he opened the flap on his ducks. He held the mug low. When it was full, he drank without pause. The taste was salt and sweet, and it was hot, but he made it cold tea, and kept it down. His tongue moved.

"Now then," said William. "Now then."

Kiminary. Keemo. Kiminary. "Keemo." Kiminary. Kiltikary. "Kiminary." Keemo. "String." Stram. Pammadilly. Lamma. Pamma. "Rat. Tag." Ring. Dong. Bomminanny. "Keemo."

He paused at each word, each word one step. The ground was lifting into woodland. His feet told him. A range of hills that were forest. He heard a far sound of roaring in his head. It seemed to be in front of him, with wisps and fast moving lumps of blue cloud that dodged here and there, jumping from behind the forest.

The sun went down red, not purple.

Lamma. Pamma. Rat. Tag.

But the dark did not come. The glow of sunset became brighter, and the sound in front of him louder. He stopped. The sky was flickering. And the whole of the tops of the hills at one instant rose as another hill, of flame. Globes of fire spun across trees, leaping gaps, and the trees exploded. The fire flowed down the hill, into a valley, showing up a nearer ridge that he had not seen. Then that ridge flared, and the fireballs danced and flew. He could hear them now, and not in his head.

William drank as he watched.

The flames were coming towards him, but moving across. If he could have run, it would not have been fast enough. The wind and the wood kindled at a speed that a horse might not outstrip. There was no choice against the flames. They were the life, and behind them, where they had been, was the night.

The wind veered, and the flames turned and sped past and to the back of him. It veered again, and encircled him. The grass and the trees marched towards him, and the fireballs danced in the tops on every side.

He coughed in the smoke. It was heavy with the smell of the church and the bee. William dug down through the dry litter to the sand until he had a hole big enough to take the mug. He wrapped the swaddledidaff in the compass, put them in the mug and buried the mug, bottom up, in the sand. He put a stone on top to mark the place, then stood to meet the fire.

Ye are the salt of the earth – daft sod. Salt.

He dragged off his shirt.

Neither do men light a candle – well, some bugger has.

He unfastened his ducks and peeled them off.

I am not come to destroy, but to fulfil – Yay. And empty barrels make most noise.

The grass rushed at him. He beat at it with both hands. It paused; came on. He beat again. But his ducks and his shirt were so worn and thin that their weight was not enough, just more food for the fire, which jumped for his hands. He let go, and the cloth was gone.

Only the speed of the burning saved him, and he danced, stamped and leapt. There was one bright flash that seared. His hair and beard crumbled.

The fireballs came from all sides and met, and their heat lifted them above William, sucking the breath from him, and above the trees into one thunder and bowled across the sky to the next stand.

He knelt. The ash was hot, no more. He moved the stone, dug into the sand and took the mug. Inside, the compass and the swaddle-didaff were unharmed.

He watched the fires move all night, until they were far off, and in the dawn he saw.

The world had changed. All around him, and away, the ground was white ash, the trees black sticks, bark charred, some smoking, some still burning. Up and down the hills there was nothing else but stick, ash, smoke, with no marks for distance or to hide the view.

William straightened the compass, grasped it with the mug in one hand, the swaddledidaff in the other, and set off.

The dust rose from his dragging feet and covered him, and each time he stumbled, charcoal made Shick-Shack again, but there were no leaves to hold against the sun.

In the dry valleys the world was walled with spikes. On the hill tops the land was wherever he looked: burnt, white, black; every tree was every tree, and there were so many: more than he could ever have thought of, under a blaze of sky that made each trunk clear and one. The land and the trees the same. Without the compass he would have been lost.

He drank the thickening liquid, and walked on.

Something moved in front of him on the ground. It was black, heaving, and changing shape. It cried out in a harsh voice. As he came near, it broke into tatters that fled in all directions and settled as crows on the trees. The noise died, and they sat, the black on the black, and watched him.

There was still something, but smaller, on the ground. William stood over it and looked.

What it had been, or what it was, he could not tell. Bones were white, and flesh, burnt and raw, with scorched fur and blistered skin stuck to them, but no shape was left, except for a toe, an eye pecked open, an ear. The guts trailed. Ants were over all.

He went to the food, not caring how he trod. His feet now were beyond the grip of their jaws. He chose a lump, a limb, something, and threw it clear. The birds watched.

He kicked it in the dust until it was free enough for him to hold and bang it on a rock to rid it of the ants. He squatted, holding with both hands, and tore, chewed, gnawed. The crows flew down to eat again. He ran at them, growling, and snatched another piece. He settled beyond where the ants swarmed; then back and to, back and to, he battled with the birds, until even they could find no more to pick and gulp. They went their ways, leaving the marrow.

It was the last. By the next day he was meeting just empty bones, ash covered in the wind.

The dust was in his mouth. There was no dew. He had to drink. He strained, but could not, trying until the muscles were dead. He threw the mug from him, and followed N.

What's that you said, young Eggy Mo? You want me for to finish the story? Then I'd best do it, or we shan't be friends, shall we? But let me ask you summat first. Where's Man in the Moon? Eh? Tell me that. He's not there, is he? Look. You show me. It's a rough auction, this, isn't it? Sun backards, moon wrong road round. And no Man. Well. Shall I tell you? There is! There is that, and all! Oh, yes. He's there, right enough! Now you do as I say. Bend over. Go on. Bend over. Right? Now look between your legs. Same as me. There. You've got it. Now look ye. He's there, isn't he? He's beggaring upside down! You'd not seen? Well I did! Close on a twelvemonth since. Whatever next, eh? I shouldn't wonder.

Now where were we? Sit thi down on that tree yonder. Tek thi bacca. Stick thi nose up chimney. Oh, yes. Henny-Penny. Going to tell king as sky's a-falling. That's it.

So they goes along and they goes along and they goes along, when who should they meet but Foxy-Woxy. Oh, I was forgetting. They'd met Turkey-Lurkey, too, but we needn't do that bit. Where are you going, Henny-Penny, Cocky-Locky, Ducky-Daddles and Turkey-Lurkey? says Foxy-Woxy. We're going to tell king the sky's a-falling.

William felt in the dark under the tree until he found a sharp stone. He broke it.

Oh, I'll come with you, says Foxy-Woxy. Snap! Hrumph! he goes. So Henny-Penny never did tell king as sky was a-falling.

And so the bridge bended. And so my tale's ended. Now, Eggy Mo, I shall have to cut thee. And he moved his arm for a vein and dragged the stone deep into him.

William sucked the blood, and sucked and licked till the flow clotted.

He could not stand. He had fallen off the trunk and lay in the ash. He held the swaddledidaff and the compass. The sun was high. He tried to move, but could not, and lay stretched out on his stomach. His arm hurt.

Het. I did me best.

He heard a yelp. He lifted his head, and saw a yellow dog standing in front of him among the trees, watching him.

Now then, Gyp.

When it knew that it had been seen, the dog turned and trotted away. William did not move. The dog stopped and looked back at him.

Gyp.

The dog whined.

It's no use.

The dog yelped again.

Gyp.

William forced himself onto his elbows.

The dog trotted off.

Wait on. Wait on.

But the dog did not stop. William pulled himself after it. In the heat, the further the dog went, the bigger it grew. William drew his knees under him, his fists closed about swaddledidaff and compass, and followed.

No dog could be so big. And now he could see the black and white hill through it. The dog filled the land and the air.

Gyp.

It was so great that he could see and not see. It did not fill the land and the air. The land and the air were it.

William reached a tree, and he stopped because his shoulder hit the trunk. It was an old tree, and above him flames still came out of the knot holes of a dead branch. He passed on; and his eye caught something above him on the other side of the trunk. It was a fresh green shoot sprouting through the blackened bark.

It were a big tree be the side o' a river. Half on it were afire, from root to top, and t'other half were green leaf all o'er. He wept. There were no tears in him to flow, but what shook him was joy.

Kil. Ki. Mo. Ti. Kar. Ki. Mo. String. Stram. Pam. Dil. Lam. Pam. Rat. Tag. Ring. Dong. Bom. Nan. Ki. Mo.

Behind him, the ash was stained as he crawled down the hill from the tree. His sight was going, but he would not stop.

He put his hand on grass: grass: alive. The dust ended in a clean line He could see a bush straight ahead, a few yards away, and on it red berries.

Kil ki mo ti kar ki mo. He was there. The berries hung above him. Whether they were poison he did not think. He reached, but he could not touch them. They glistened.

He felt among the grass. He put the compass in his other hand, crawled beneath the branches until he could grasp the stem, and shook it. He shook it with all his little strength. He heard dropping in the grass. He let go of the trunk and swept his hand around. His fingers touched a smoothness and picked it up and held it close to his face. Red. A berry. He put it in his mouth; and bit.

Under the skin, the flesh was soft. The taste was like nothing ever: new, yet a memory; a dream woken.

He found more berries, ate them, without shaking the stem again. He had no need. All to be done now was to go.

He raised his head. His sight had cleared. He was beside a dry river, two tall trees together on the other side. He looked up. A bird was above him, spread on the sky.

He hauled himself to the river and slid head first down. He crossed the bed, taking no care of the stones and the tangled branches. He climbed the bank with the last force of his mind; and then before him were only the trees, and beyond and between them a low hillock, and, upright on the hillock, a dead sapling.

Yon's a right stick for to take a man home.

He crawled past the trees and onto the hillock. At the top, he grabbed the sapling with one hand. The big bird hovered.

Oss off. I'm none of your baggin.

He pulled, but he was too weak even to lift to his knees, and he swung round, hanging from his arm. The compass fell, and the wind caught it.

He was facing the two trees. On the side of each, opposite the hillock, a slice of bark had been cut away, and deep in the wood were the patterns on the timbers of the barn, the shapes of Mutlow: lines, curved and crooked; dots, spots and twisted circles; but not shimmering; all still, weathered, real.

Bloody no. I said. Bloody no.

Darkness rolled upwards across his eyes.

Lu lay, lu lay, lu lara lay; bayu, bayu, lu lara lay; hush-a-bye, lu lay. And the fruit of that forbidden tree, whose mortal taste brought death into the world, and all our woe, with loss of Eden. Man of leaf and golden hood. We mun wake him if we could.

There was wet on his face.

Cush, cush. Cush-a-cush. And the leaves of the tree were for the healing of the nations.

He opened his eyes. A dog stood over him. Someone was sitting on the ground before the hillock, a big willow leaf in his hair, made of red wood.

William spoke.

"Are we at China, then?"

[120]

IV

MURRANGURK

Fro spot my spyryt þer sprang in space;
My body on balke þer bod. In sweuen
My goste is gon in Godez grace,
In auenture þer meruaylez meuen

"Pearl"
lines 61/5

19

Nullamboin smelt the wind. He sat by his fire. The wind was blowing dust and leaves. A piece of bark dropped in front of him. He reached with the butt of his spear and pulled the bark over and lifted it, and smelt. He looked at the lines painted on it: the cross of life in the circle of Being of the People; above, the mark of the three toes of the hallowed bird; above, the crooked path of travel, from the holy to the holy. He put the bark into the medicine bag that was slung at his shoulder. Then he took red clay and painted a band of red across his eyes, a band of red across his nose and cheek bones, two lines down the middle of his chest, turning along the bottom ribs, and, outside each of these lines, two shorter ones that did not turn. With his other hand he took white clay, and ran white dots around the lines. On his legs he drew in white the solemn path of the snake, and marked its fires with a dot in the curve of each bend. When this was done, he gathered his spears and walked away. His kal followed him.

Nullamboin went to the Place of Growing, beyond the fires. He scooped water out of the Spirit Hole and drank. Then he sat by the Spirit Hole and sang the songs of the Ancestor and of the Dreaming to the son of Bunjil, Binbeal, the Rainbow, who lived in the waters.

Then he sat before the Goomah, the Clashing Rock, and he sang his spirit into the rock until he was safe. Next, he stood and went to the hollow Minggah, and reached inside the tree and lifted out a bag of kowir skin and opened it. In the bag were the churingas of wood that held all his Dreamings. He took the red churinga of the Kal

Dreaming, and fixed it in the back of his headband, and danced the life of the Place of Growing into him, and left.

He came to the grave mound. A man lay, gripping the spear that had been put there. Nullamboin sat down and looked to the sky. An eagle soared above the two trees. He waited. The man groaned, and the kal went to him and licked his face; and the man opened his eyes and spoke, then his head dropped forward. The kal whined. Nullamboin crossed the trench and bent to smell the man's face and breathing. He uncurled the fist that was holding the stone all stuck about with crystal that shone in the light. He took the stone into his medicine bag, and held the man hard by the upper arms for a moment, then turned and walked back to the Place of Growing. His kal lay at the mound.

He pulled the churinga from his headband and laid it in the Minggah, and sat before the Clashing Rock and sang his spirit out to him. He danced the life back into the Place of Growing, then he went to the fires.

Nullamboin sat, and stared far off, his spears beside him, his hands on his thighs, fingers spread.

All the elders looked up.

Woolmurgen came to sit by Nullamboin.

Marrowuk joined them.

Bundurang came; and Mamaluga; Punmuttal; Konkontallin. Derrimut moved towards them, but Nullamboin brought the back of his hand to his face, and swung his arm forward and out to the side, and Derrimut stopped, and went to his fire.

Nullamboin reached into his medicine bag and took out the piece of bark and gave it to the men. They each smelt it in turn, and looked at the lines painted on it: the cross of life in the circle of Being of the People; above, the mark of the three toes of the hallowed bird; above, the crooked path of travel, from the holy to the holy.

"It is a sacred journey of the Kowir Dreaming come to us," said Mamaluga.

"Death has died into life here at our Place of Growing," said Woolmurgen.

"And a greater Dreaming has come," said Punmuttal.

Bundurang nodded and gave the bark to Nullamboin; and Nullamboin put it into his mouth, chewed, and swallowed.

"You danced that it would come."

Nullamboin looked at him.

"No one has danced this before," said Bundurang.

Nullamboin looked at him. "When the sky falls, the People shall not die in their Dreaming." He picked up his spears, and the men went with him, carrying theirs. They made towards the Place of Growing.

"There is no harm," said Nullamboin, and led them straight to the grave mound.

When they saw what was on it, and the hand holding, they sat, and turned their eyes to the side.

"It doesn't look like him," said Marrowuk. "Too big."

"It's a young man, not mulla-mullung," said Woolmurgen.

"Why is it that colour?" said Konkontallin. "The dead are white."

"Never as he was will he return," said Nullamboin. "He died before his song was sung, before his step in the Dance was ended."

Nullamboin showed the crystal stone.

"Here is his thundal."

He put it back in the medicine bag, and stood, and the others joined him, shuffling, uncertain, until Nullamboin painted the red bands across their eyes and cheeks. On their legs he drew in white the solemn path of the snake, and marked its fires with a dot in the curve of each bend. Given their strength, the men became still.

"After I had danced, I sang," said Nullamboin. "I sang him in the

Kal Dreaming. And, as I dreamed, I saw him dancing in the Minggah of Tharangalkbek, by the Spirit Hole of Tharangalkbek, and there were many dead people. But the Goomah of Tharangalkbek I could not see clear, for there the Goomah is Women's Matter. That is strange.

"I sent the Kal Dreaming into his kal, and it took him. And the dead people wrapped him in the net of Death and Life, and washed him in the Spirit Hole, so that he might walk the Hard Darkness, and ride the Bone of the Cloud, to come to us."

Nullamboin pointed at the sky, and, when they saw the eagle above them, the elders cried out.

"Bunjil!"

"The Father-of-our-Flesh gives his eagle to tell you this," said Nullamboin. "This man is mulla-mullung. He has forgotten, but he will remember. Do not be afraid. Bunjil gives him his eagle. The strong singer claims his spear. Murrangurk has come."

"It is as you danced," said Bundurang. "Kah."

"Take him," said Nullamboin. "The net is thin, and must mend with blood, and honey, and bwal, and gunyeru. Take him to the fires."

The men stamped, and danced, and with their spears they gashed their arms and chests, so that their life flowed for the man before them; and Bundurang, and Marrowuk, and Mamaluga and Kon-kontallin went to the mound and took him on their shoulders and laid his spear over him, letting their life run along him, so that the net would hold. They danced with him towards the fires, singing his Kal Dreaming, lest he should die again.

The women heard the song, and they sang their grief at his long going from them. They tore their hair to let free their power for him, and ripped their flesh to give him life, putting their firesticks to the blood to make it spirit for him, and, singing, they went out to meet the men and to bring him home.

But Purranmurnin Tallarwurnin stayed by her fire, and mixed water, and honey, and wallundunderren gum with her hands; and when the men came they laid him by her, and she put his head in her lap and let the yellow trickle from her fingers to his lips.

He did not move. She stroked his mouth. His lips opened, and she fed him slowly from her fingers, while the women sang and the men danced, to hold him and make good the net.

The men and women left. Purranmurnin Tallarwurnin took a shell, and with its point and edge she cut the maggots from the sores of his body and burnt them, and cleaned the sores with bwal sap. He cried out, and slept.

The men built a tall fire at either end of the Place of Growing, and when that was done they covered their bodies with kowir fat and rubbed it in. Then they painted each other with white clay: circles around the eyes, for the sacred ground, lines along the brow, down the nose, one down the cheeks, to the chin; lines on the arms, the chest, to the stomach; from the stomach to the legs and feet; so that the spirit would run from the earth to the centre, and from the still centre to the eye, and the eye send it out.

As the night came, they lit the fires, and went to gather branches of green bwal. They tied bwal about their arms and ankles, and Nullamboin put fresh red clay on his headband, and kowir feathers around it, and plover in his hair.

The men passed from the firelight into the dark, and the women carried the man and laid him before them, and sat around the edge of the Place of Growing, their wolard skin cloaks rolled tightly and held across their thighs.

They beat the rolled cloaks, which sounded under their hands in rhythm; and from the darkness the men came stamping into the light, carrying long clubs, and sticks that they beat to answer the women's drums with the rustling bwal.

They sang, and played and danced on the ground that was hard with the stain of blood and life. Below the ground, the earth boomed in the hollow logs that were buried there. And in the shadow of the flames they sang, and played and danced gunyeru for the man that had come to them, giving his spirit all their spirit, dancing towards him with the bwal branches high, brushing the ground, and back; the clapsticks speaking the voice of air; the drums and the feet speaking the voice of earth, and the power of the ground rising through the limbs, kept at the centre, cast from the eyes.

The man was awake, and watched. Nullamboin left the dance and went to him. The man spoke, but Nullamboin slung a bag of woven hair over the man's shoulder and under his arm, showed him the crystal stone glinting rainbows of fire so that no one else could see, and put it in the bag and went back to the dance.

Through that night the People held his spirit, until their strength was gone. But the sky paled, and their strength came back to dance for the Morning Star. And, at the frenzy, the men raised their clubs and shouted with one voice. "Mami-ngata!"

Silence. Gunyeru was done.

Nullamboin, sweating, looked at a woman, and she held the man and set her running breast to his mouth. The man fed.

20

They put him on a rug under a shelter of bark, and Purranmurnin Tallarwurnin came and lay against his front, pulling the rug over them both. He smelt woman's smell, but it was different: part rank, part musk; and the skin was velvet. A dog lay along his back to keep him warm. He moved in and out of sleep, until the fingers stroked his lips again, and the liquid was in his mouth, sweet as honey, mixed with a sharpness, as strong as turkey rhubarb, vinegar, sour. The fingers pushed between his teeth and rubbed the flow onto his tongue. The fingers went and came back, again and again, until the taste was comfort, and life was in his throat. He felt the crystal through the net.

When he woke, he was alone. Across from him, old men with grey hair were sitting on their folded legs and talking beside a fire. At another fire, old women worked and laughed. Some children were playing.

He watched and dozed. All day, a man or a woman would check that there was water in the bowl beside him; but, except for that, they took no notice.

As the sun dropped, the younger men appeared, tired and dusty, with only their weapons in their hands. Soon the women came, chattering and laughing, with babies on their backs, and bags filled with roots and berries, and small, dead animals. They were followed by children, who dragged wood for the fires.

The day became busy night. Food was made ready, and, after they had eaten, they sang and danced, until the end, when the People turned to their fires and slept, and Purranmurnin Tallarwurnin gave

William more of the yellow gum and lay beside him, the dog behind.

So each morning he watched the men leave, in silence, carrying spears and shields and curved pieces of wood; and the women would wander off more slowly, holding pointed sticks, and always talking, always laughing.

Sometimes the men came back with fish and eels, and sometimes they had things that he had never seen, so big that it took two men to carry them. Then there was shouting, and a special fire was made, and the animal was thrown into the flames to singe the fur or the feathers, and it was pulled off the fire, raw and charred, and cut into pieces with stone and shared with all. But he was given none. For him, the old men and women made a different food, and fed him small pieces through the day.

After they had all eaten, they sang and danced: different songs, different dances, different patterns on their bodies. And the songs and the dances made William stronger than did the water he drank or the food he ate, and the strength stayed with him.

"Eh! Taffy!"

The old men looked up.

"Taffy! Fetch us some baggin!"

A man came to the shelter and checked the water bowl. He said something.

"Nay. Is that all they learn you?"

The man made more sound.

"Give over mollocking. All yon 'yanna-koojalla' nominy! Can you not talk like a Christian?"

The man went to a woman. She put handfuls into a shallow dish and pummelled with a stick and gave the dish to the man. He brought it. Inside was a paste with small pieces that were dark and hard, and the paste looked like a flesh.

"What's this tack? I've never seen owt of that afore."

The man spoke, and pointed to his mouth, and went back to

the other men.

He sniffed.

I doubt there's not much cop here.

But he was hungry, and he took some of the paste on his finger and sucked it. It was a kind of meat, and there were juices, yet it tasted of nut: a rich, sticky nut. He ate more. Well. None so bad. He scooped out the dish. There had been only a little, but it was enough. As he swallowed the last lump, a part of it twitched.

What he liked best was to watch the children who stayed behind, the sun golden on their yellow hair. The girls played cat's cradle; and the boys played at being men.

The men had their pieces of bent wood, and so had the boys. They would stand and hold the wood by one end, behind their head, and throw it over their shoulder. It spun away in a line, and then turned and looped in all directions: right, left, up, down; and then it would hover, twirling like a sycamore key, and, still spinning, come back to the thrower, so that it fell at his feet; and, just before it fell, it hung still in the air. And every flight was different, and every drop the same.

One boy stood, and the rest were quiet. He made his throw, and watched it all the way; and, at the moment when it hung above him, and the spin that would have broken his hand stopped, before it fell, he reached up and took hold of the wood at the centre of its curve. And the other boys danced and cheered.

Well, I'll go to Buxton!

Forgetting that he was too weak to move, he got up and walked out from the shelter towards the boys.

An old man spoke, and they scattered, except for the boy who had just thrown.

"Hey! Now then, Dick-Richard! Whoever learnt you to do like yon?"

The boy put out a hand and touched him, then smelt his fingers. He moved forward and looked up, offering the curved wood.

"Wangim," he said. "Wangim."

"Oh, crimes!"

The boy's eyes were covered with a white film.

"Wangim."

"You conner see!"

"Ongee. Wangim."

The boy felt for his hand and put the bent wood in it, then pointed.

"Wangim."

"Wangim?"

The children clapped and shouted: "Wangim! Wangim!"

"Right, mester, right! Four nobles a year's a crown a quarter! My song! Let's give it some fullock, shall us?"

He held the wood as best as he could remember, and threw it hard. It tumbled straight and clattered into a tree. The children screamed with laughter, and even the old men and women joined in. Someone ran to fetch the wangim, for him to throw again. But he was gripping the boy by the shoulders, and looking at his eyes.

"Nay," he said. "If you can thole, what's up with me?"

"Wangim?"

He let go of the boy.

"Not wangim, youth. China."

He was unsteady, but he could manage. Nobody tried to stop him. He did not know which way was north, but he could make a compass later. He set off away from where the hunters had gone. One of the old men put his hands on his thighs, and hummed softly, deep in his chest, and the note did not pause or change as he breathed.

He kept going. The giddiness left him, but he often had to rest. Yet he kept going. He was in the great silence, and, since all looked the same, he tried to walk forwards, so that he would not wander and come back. He had seen how the men walked, one foot in front of another, not to the side, unwavering. He did the same, slowly, but that did not matter, so long as he moved on.

He would be hungry. He would have to thirst. But he had lived before, and now there was food, and there was water, if he could find them, and, because of that, the land was not empty, and he was not afraid. And even in the great silence he was not alone. The ground would not let him fall. His foot spoke the earth, and made it new, now and in its beginning; and that earth spoke him now, new, in step and breath that met in its dance, so that the ground and the man sang as one. To China, all the way.

"Cooo-ee!"

The cry was behind him.

"Cooo-ee!"

To the side.

He looked. Four men trotted in and out among the trees, carrying spears and shields.

"Oss off! Oss off!"

He tried to run, but he had forgotten how, and when he moved faster, the earth did not listen, and would not hear. And he, deaf as before, stumbled, the song out of tune.

"Cooo-ee!"

The four caught up with him and surrounded him, but did not take hold of him. He had to stop.

"Damn yer to hell!" He was crying. "Leave me be! Oss bloody off! I'm going home!"

But they were crying, too. The tears were on their cheeks. They tapped his chest briefly, as if fearful, and thumped their own, then beckoned and pointed back the way he had come.

He moved to pass them, but they blocked him, still not touching, still crying.

He fell on his knees, and the men stood over him, in anguish.

"Het! It's no use! Het! I tried! It's no use! Het! They'll not let me!"

21

He was dreaming; and he knew that he was dreaming. He lay under the rug, and the woman in front of him, the dog behind. But he was dreaming.

The men had brought him back to the fires, still not touching him, not even to help him when the weakness slowed his step, but smiling, laughing, still at the edge of tears. They had taken him to his shelter, and the woman had given him water. She had come back from her gathering to be with him, and she stayed all day to feed and comfort him.

Then, after the dancing, she had drawn the rug over them, and slept.

They were asleep now, he knew. But he was dreaming. He was dreaming the fires, and the sleepers, all as they were.

The man with feathers in his hair, who had given him the woven bag for the swaddledidaff, came towards him. He was painted with red clay, and he looked down into his eyes, then turned and walked. He followed him. Neither the dog nor the woman moved.

They walked among the trees far beyond the firelight, under the moon, and came to a lake. Near it was a rock, and beside the lake a tree grew, away from the other trees, and, though it was not tall, its trunk was wider than its crown.

In front of the rock sat the old men, in a circle, and all were painted with the red clay. They sang, and clapped the ringing sticks together. The man led him into the circle and painted him as the men, and then stood him before the rock. He forced his right hand open against the stone, and sprayed red clay over it with his mouth. The print of the hand was sharp on the stone. The man wound a net about his head, so that he could not see, and held him by the arms from behind.

The old men stopped their song, but still beat the sticks, slowly, and the echo of them bounced off the rock and grew louder, until the rock itself was ringing, and he could no longer hear the sticks behind him, but only the clashing of the rock before. He felt the hands on his shoulders tighten, and they moved him into a balance, holding him, and then, at a pause between the echo, he was shoved forward, and would have fallen, but for the hands, and the echo was behind him, then silent everywhere.

The hands unwound the net. He was inside the rock, and the old men were sitting in a circle, and the walls and roof and floor were all of shining crystals.

He turned around. There was no way out of the cave. He was in a skep of brightness and humming light.

Each crystal fitted the next, though they were of different size and shape, but he saw that they had five sides. Even the smallest made a clunch of five.

But the wall was not right. There was a hole. He went to it and touched it; yet, though he could see the hole, he could not put his fingers in. The air would not yield.

He looked at the man. The man looked at him. He looked again at the hole. He knew the shape. It was not five sides, but an egg, rough, and black. There was no moon outside, but the black was full of stars, and it was not one sky but many, bubbled as a brain, and every sky had stars, and the stars were of the humming.

He took the swaddledidaff from the bag at his shoulder and placed it against the hole. The shape fitted, and the air held it. The swaddle-didaff left no gap; the wall was made.

He looked at the man again. The man reached forward and pulled out the swaddledidaff and gave it back to him, closing the hand about it. There was no hole in the wall.

He put the swaddledidaff in his bag. The brightness and the humming grew, and the rock parted. The man dragged him between the gap, and the clash of its shutting was behind them. The old men sat, silent, in the moonlight.

He went and lay in the circle, on his back, and the man knelt and took his head between his knees. He gripped the flesh of the middle of the nostrils with his finger and thumb and dribbled his own spit onto it, while the old men sang again to the clapsticks, but this a song of happiness; and, when the flesh was slippery and loose, the man thrust a sharp bone through the nose, turning the bone until he had pushed it to its thickest point; then he slid it out and stuck a wooden peg in as far as the peg's middle, so that the ends were level with the side of the mouth.

The man held the peg at either end, and lifted him to his feet, and led him to the tree.

The tree was hollow, and the man moved him against the bark, and he felt himself sink into the bark. He could hear the men and the ringing sticks.

There was light in the tree. It came from the bodies of snakes that covered the inside so that the wood was hidden. They twined about each other, and their light was the coloured fires of the swaddle-didaff, and they twined about him: his feet, and legs, and arms, and hands and body, and their curling lifted him. He looked, but there was no crown to the tree; only an open pillar of snakes rising upward and lifting him with them. The song and the music faded and he was carried by the writhing light that breathed and whispered and was dry and rippled along and about him and in him, becoming his bones, his throat, his veins and all his being, an endless tree of light, of snakes, of a man borne to the sky. Until there was the egg of the cave, one sky, now smooth, both tips round the same, and no stars.

The sky grew bigger as he was carried up, and then it was all that there was above him, dark, and the coiling lifted him against it, and it was hard. Yet though it had no beginning, and no depth, there was a pattern carved upon it: five lines inside each other of diamond pane, and, in the pane, six rings with one middle; but he could not feel them as his face was pressed against the sky and it was hard.

He tried to shout, but he made no sound. And this was death. He knew. Fingers took him by the peg on either side and drew him into the darkness, through the rings, through darkness that clung as black as earth, and into light.

He was in the oak, beside the mere, below the Hamestan, under the moon. Grandad held him by the peg with one hand.

He sat on his legs, as the men did, and from each shoulder a crystal went up the sky, and to them there was no ending.

"Eh! On your shoulders, Grandad. Whatever is it?"

"That's for thee to see, and me to know," said Grandad.

He woke. He reached for the comfort of the woman, but there was nothing. He started to fall, and his other arm held him. It was morning, and he lay on a branch of the hollow tree. Below him sat the men.

His face hurt, and he tasted blood at the back of his throat. He lifted his hand. His nose was swollen, and through the middle of it he felt a wooden peg. The men sang and clapped their sticks.

He looked at his body. It was painted all over red.

~~~~~~~~~~

22

Murrangurk stood on the shore of Beangala in the Dulur country. He scratched the sand with his spear, making marks. Het. He turned his head and looked at them and scratched again. Het. Beside him, his kal sat, watching. Murrangurk tasted dust and charred wood in his mouth.

He felt Nullamboin speak to him, and looked up. Nullamboin was sitting under a tree. What are you doing? I smell burnt food.

I smell nothing, uncle.

Nullamboin walked down to the shore. His kal followed him. He looked at the scratches.

"Why do you cut sand?"

"I am seeing."

"But why cut sand?"

"I am seeing."

"That does not make you cut sand."

"It is a word," said Murrangurk.

"I don't hear it," said Nullamboin.

"It is a word seen." He scratched again. "Het."

"That is not a word."

"It is a name," said Murrangurk.

"A name? What name?"

"A woman."

"No woman is called 'Het'! There is no Het among the Beingalite. It is not Wurunjerri-baluk, or Bunurong, or Kurung, or Gunung-

Willam, or Jajaurung, or Wotjobaluk, or Gournditch-Mara. Who speaks Het? Where did you hear it?"

"I can't see," said Murrangurk. "It is from before."

"When you are dead?"

Murrangurk looked at the water.

"I dreamed her: in Tharangalkbek."

"What was her name and her People before she died?" said Nullamboin.

"She wasn't dead," said Murrangurk.

"She was mulla-mullung woman?"

"No. She did not come by the Rainbow or the Hard Darkness. It was her country."

"No man, no woman, is called Het," said Nullamboin. "It is not a name."

"I dreamed her," said Murrangurk.

"That is no need to cut sand," said Nullamboin.

"It will make the word stay."

Nullamboin breathed through his nose and looked at Murrangurk.

"If you cut sand?"

"Yes."

"If you cut bark?"

"Yes."

"Wood?"

"Yes."

"Rock?"

"Yes."

"Can it be drawn?"

"Yes."

"Show me 'Mami-ngata'."

Murrangurk scratched the sand.

"That is 'Mami-ngata'?" said Nullamboin.

STRANDLOPER

"Yes."

"Show me his big name."

Murrangurk scratched 'Bunjil'.

"That is 'Bunjil'?"

"Yes."

Nullamboin shouted, and rubbed out the mark with his foot.

"Is it still there?"

"No," said Murrangurk.

"But you could cut it, in another place, and it could stay? In wood or rock?"

"Yes. It is how to make words."

"And it would be for those to see, if they came, or it could be carried far off and seen by strangers."

"It could."

"So any girl, or woman, or boy that has not been Smoked, or young man will be able to speak as elders and mulla-mullung?"

He took a crystal from his bag.

"What is this for those who do not Dream?"

Murrangurk scratched 'wallung'.

"Wallung?"

Murrangurk nodded.

"Now the flesh name."

Murrangurk scratched.

"Thundal?" said Nullamboin.

"Thundal, uncle."

Nullamboin cried out and rubbed the sand. He turned, his kal at his heels, and strode away.

"Then all will see without knowledge, without teaching, without dying into life! Weak men will sing! Boys will have eagles! All shall be mad! Why have I danced this thing?"

"Uncle!"

[140]

Murrangurk hurried after him. His kal stayed by the marks.

A wave washed in from the sea, and Het was gone. The kal followed the men.

"Uncle! We must go to the fires! A wordholder is coming!"

"I don't feel him," said Nullamboin.

"You are angry," said Murrangurk. "But my shoulder tells me."

Nullamboin changed direction, and they ran.

The women and the young men were returning home, and Brairnumin was with them. He was helping to carry the body of a kowir. As Murrangurk and Nullamboin reached them, he called out to Murrangurk, "I heard him, uncle, and my wangim broke his leg, ki! Warrowil speared him, hai! Light the fire!" His filmed eyes were shining stones.

"A wordholder is coming. He has crossed the Barwin," said Murrangurk.

The women and children went to their shelters. The young men stood with their weapons. And the elders sat facing towards the river, and waited.

The sun was going into its hole when a man appeared, walking. He carried a green branch of peace, one spear and a shield.

At a distance from the warriors, he sat, and made himself a small fire. Koronn, Nullamboin's wife, came from her shelter and laid branches on the elders' fire, and went back to her place. No one spoke. Then, when the waters had risen between them all, the man got up and entered.

The young men put down their weapons. The man who had come went with Nullamboin to the elders' fire and talked quietly. The other elders sat apart.

"He is Tirrawal, of the Kurung," said Derrimut.

"He is the Crow brother of the sister of the mother of Koronn," said Murrangurk.

[141]

When the men had talked at the fire, Nullamboin called the People to him, and they sat and listened.

"In the Beginning," said Nullamboin, "when the waters parted and the Ancestors Dreamed all that is, and woke the life that slept, the sky lay on the earth, and the sun could not move, until the Magpie lifted the sky with a stick."

"A stick!" said the listeners.

"And when the Dreaming was done, and each Ancestor made of himself churinga, Mami-ngata had strong poles of bwal set around the sky; and he put the Old Man to look after them and keep them firm, so that the sky should not fall."

"Not fall!"

"Then Mami-ngata trod upon the whirlwind and rode beyond the Bone of the Cloud, and he sits in Tharangalkbek to look upon the living and to guide the dead."

"The dead!"

"Now Tirrawal, Crow brother of the sister of the mother of Koronn, brings dreams."

"Brings dreams!"

"The mulla-mullung of the Mogullumbitch and of the Ballung-Karar say that the Old Man comes to them, and they dream that the poles of bwal beyond their country have rotted and must be made new."

"Made new!"

"The Old Man says they must send wordholders through all the peoples of the world, even as far as the Kerinma and the Gournditch-Mara, to make axes, so that he may cut bwal and save the sky. If he does not have the axes, the sky will fall."

"Will fall!"

The women began to wail and the men to shout.

"We have no axes to give," said Derrimut. "How shall we build our fires without wood?"

"If the sky falls, there will be no fires," said Nullamboin.

"Without axes, how shall we carve the trees of the dead?" said Murrangurk. "How shall they sing their Dreamings and make their spirit ways?"

"If the sky falls, there will be none to die," said Nullamboin.

"Then where will be our Dreaming?" said Murrangurk.

"There will be no Dreaming," said Nullamboin.

"The elders and mulla-mullung must talk of this," said Murrangurk.

The young men and the boys stripped the kowir of its feathers and skin, and Nullamboin cut pieces of flesh from the front of the legs and from the back of the thighs and wrapped them in leaves, so that the flesh could be not touched. Brairnumin took the leaves to Murrangurk.

"Eat, uncle. Here is your kowir. It is time for the fire."

Murrangurk blackened his face and sides with charcoal before touching the raw meat that the blind young man put onto the ground, then the bird was taken out to the new fire, so that the women should not see, and the body cut open and parted with flint. Each time a bone was broken, the men gave a shout, and when the flesh and guts were hot, they were brought back. The best piece and the fat were given in honour to Tirrawal. The men rubbed charcoal into their faces and sides before eating the sacred bird, but few spoke, and after, there was no sound but the sob of women and the murmur of the men.

The elders talked through the night of the dreams that Tirrawal had brought, until the sky awoke. The rug drums and the clapsticks were silent, and the People could not be lifted to song. Murrangurk alone, in the unburnt spirit of kowir, danced the Morning Star.

23

Tirrawal went back to his country, and wordholders were sent to the Kaurn-kopan, to the Peek-wurong, the Mukjarawaint and to the Jupa Galk. The elders met, and they decided the talk of the night.

"If the sky should fall now," said Derrimut, "the waters would come to cover the land. We shall move to the highest of our ground, and our fires will burn on Morriock in two nights."

"We must send to the Kurnaje-berring to talk with Billi-billeri for the stone of Bomjinna," said Murrangurk. "Who is to go?"

"Gambeech and Warrowil are of the same skins by their mothers," said Nullamboin.

"Shall both go?"

"Send Gambeech," said Nullamboin. "He is the man who knows stone. And give him wolard and kowir bags made by Purranmurnin Tallarwurnin to show. Her thread is the strongest."

The People moved without noise. Now they were less troubled. To walk the land would give them life, and the land would be made again by their tread. It might hold the sky.

Murrangurk pulled down the bark of their shelter. Purranmurnin Tallarwurnin had gathered her rugs and bowls and her digging stick and smoothed the fire.

"We are to talk with Billi-billeri for the stone of Bomjinna," said Murrangurk. "Give me a bag of wolard and a bag of kowir skin to send."

"I can't find them all," said Purranmurnin Tallarwurnin. "There has been a thief."

"Who of the Beingalite would steal?" said Murrangurk. "Are your eyes dim?"

"Not my eyes that are dim," said Purranmurnin Tallarwurnin.

Murrangurk looked at her, and she was laughing.

"Why would my nephew do that?" said Murrangurk. "I have taught him the stories of the Beginning, and the names of his flesh spirits and those of the People. I am leading him through the ways of his Dreaming, and I led him to be made a man and held him when he was Smoked. How have I done him wrong that he should steal?"

Purranmurnin Tallarwurnin put her hand on his cheek. He was crying.

"He is sad that he may not stand with the warriors."

"I may not fight. Yet I do not steal."

"Your Dreaming is greater. You must not die again into death. Brairnumin does not steal. He tries to show you that he is a warrior, though he stays with the women in battle."

Murrangurk walked outside, in a circle, looking at the ground.

Hah.

He raised his head, and sniffed. Then he followed the marks that he had seen. They were straight, and he knew them. He lifted his head again and judged their line by the sun.

Fool.

He ran back. The People were ready. Gambeech was with Nullamboin. Murrangurk went to them.

"Where are the wolard and kowir bags, uncle?" said Gambeech.

"Kah!"

Murrangurk took the light shield that Gambeech carried, and the reed spear with the man's belt and the woman's apron hanging from it. He bound red cord about his arms below the shoulder, for strength, and put fresh red upon his headband.

"What are you doing, nephew?" said Nullamboin. "Have you a

ghost in you? Where are the bags?"

"The ghost is not in me," shouted Murrangurk. "It has the mind of Brairnumin; and he has taken two bags and a wolard skin. I have seen his feet! And if I can't stop him, he is dead."

"What is he doing?"

"He is walking towards the Wurunjerri-baluk, to be a wordholder to the Kurnaje-berring for Bomjinna stone, so that we may call him warrior! But he does not know the signs of the Wurunjerri-baluk! He thinks that he can be wordholder of peace without spear and belt and apron!"

"You are not kindred," said Nullamboin. "It was not for this that I danced and sang."

"I carry the signs that are true," said Murrangurk. "No one can harm them."

"There is danger on such a journey from our country," said Nullamboin. "I smell blood."

"When I see the feet of Brairnumin," Murrangurk sang, "I smell blood. But it is the blood and fire and tearing of my dance, of my song, of my Dreaming, and I must go; or without earth is your dance, and silent your song, and empty your Dreaming."

Murrangurk left his kal and followed the tracks out of the camp. Brairnumin had fallen twice and had grazed his leg on a tree, but he was travelling well, keeping his way by the feel of the sun. Murrangurk trotted quietly. Brairnumin would not be far ahead, and he did not want to frighten the young man so that he hurt himself.

He had stood, and, though the sand had dried, the smell was still strong. Murrangurk walked, making no sound. He came upon a water scrape that was damp, and he had to scoop only once to be able to drink for himself. Now he listened. He could not see any distance, because of the scrub and hummocks of rough ground.

He listened. Ahead of him he heard what he knew he would find:

the steady click click of wangim being knocked together. He moved gently. Around the next dune he saw Brairnumin, two bags on his shoulders, one filled with a rug; his head turned, smelling, and hearing, guided by the sand and the changing echoes of the tapping wood.

Nephew.

Brairnumin stopped.

Uncle.

Where are you going?

To Bomjinna, to ask the great man Billi-billeri to let us take stone for axes to stop the sky from falling. I have wolard and kowir skins to show him what we can bring.

And do you speak Wurunjerri-baluk?

I am a wordholder in peace, and wordholders are sacred.

How will you find Bomjinna?

My brother of my Smoking, the Crow, will tell me.

Why did you not ask the elders before you left?

You would not have let me go. You think that I cannot see. But it is only my eyes that are blind.

Will you let me come? said Murrangurk. Two wordholders and warriors together?

It would please me, said Brairnumin.

And I, too, should be pleased, said Murrangurk.

He put the young man's hand on his shield to guide him, and they walked for Bomjinna.

After two days, they came in the evening towards a river, not as big as others they had crossed.

I see some water, said Brairnumin.

We shall stay on this side, said Murrangurk. On the other is Wurunjerri-baluk land. It will be a cold night. We must not light a fire.

I am not cold, said Brairnumin.

They slept, and, with the Morning Star, Murrangurk searched up the river bank until he found a hollow dead tree. It had three big branches, with holes in them. He took mud from the river and stopped up the holes of one of the branches. Then he took dry and damp grass and made a fire inside the tree, so that the smoke came out of the other two branches.

What are you doing, uncle? said Brairnumin. Why is there fire in a tree? Are we to catch wolard?

I am speaking to the Wurunjerri-baluk, said Murrangurk.

Murrangurk sat on the river bank and watched the trees along the tops of the hills. He put more damp grass on the fire.

Shall we cross now? said Brairnumin. I feel the warm sun.

No, said Murrangurk, and watched.

Now we cross, said Murrangurk.

Two columns of smoke were rising from a tree on the skyline.

Murrangurk and Brairnumin swam the river, and walked all day up into the hills. The ground became more broken and wooded, until they were in forest.

As the light died, Murrangurk said, We must find their shelters. Tell me when you see fire.

It is the length of sunset over there, said Brairnumin, and they will eat a male koim tonight.

Soon even Murrangurk could smell the burning wood, and when he saw light through the trees he stopped and put his hand on Brairnumin's lips. He lifted the shield and tapped it four times with the butt of the spear, paused, and tapped again twice. He waited, listening. There was silence. Then came answering taps: four, and two.

Murrangurk and Brairnumin went forwards, careful not to be silent. The light fell upon them, and they sat. When the waters had risen, they entered, Murrangurk holding the decorated spear high before him.

A voice spoke from the fire.

"Murrangurk, it is a long time since the wind blew the mark of your steps away."

24

From the fires the track led them upwards, always upwards, into forest where the trees grew taller, and the light was fainter, and cloud drifted everywhere. They shivered with the dank. And then the cloud was small rain, and wind blew gently and cold and quiet.

Murrangurk raised the spear of the wordholder upright, so that it was the first thing for anyone to see, and they trod on sticks that snapped.

There are men, said Brairnumin with his body.

Do not be afraid, said Murrangurk.

They climbed all day, and the ground became stony, with black rocks lying among the leaves.

Brairnumin felt them with his feet.

We are in the axe country, he said.

Do not touch them with your hand, said Murrangurk.

They ate the food that had been given to them at the fires, but they took nothing from the forest that could be eaten.

They came to black cliffs, and walked along the sides and up into them by cracks.

Stop, said Murrangurk.

He tapped the shield with the spear: four and two. He waited.

Sit.

They sat, and did not speak; and the mountain looked at them through gaps in the cloud that the wind blew, and it was big over them and they were cold.

Murrangurk lowered his head, and made Brairnumin do the same. The light was fading, and darkness came out of Bomjinna.

Above them, far above them, they heard the tap of a spear: four and two. Brairnumin and Murrangurk stood, and climbed.

There are fires, said Brairnumin. All the People are waiting, and the rain is on their shelters.

Brairnumin and Murrangurk reached the top of the crack. In front of them the rock was flat, and on it were fires inside the openings of the shelters. A man wearing a cloak of wolard came to meet them and took them to a shelter where there were two elders, one the age of Murrangurk, the other wrinkled and with hair all white. This man smoothed the ground with his hand, and said, "I am glad to see you, Murrangurk, but you must be gentle and hurt no one and speak straight."

The other man repeated the words just as the old man had said them, but he was standing.

Murrangurk sat on the cleared ground, and put Brairnumin beside him. Every man of the camp was painted white.

"I am glad to see you, Billi-billeri," he said. "And I have brought you a wolard rug, and would talk of the wolard and the kowir bags that I also bring."

"I know why you would talk," said Billi-billeri, "and this is Bungerim of the Wurunjerri-baluk of Jara-wait who gives my word."

And Bungerim spoke again everything that Billi-billeri had spoken.

"You have come to talk stone of Bomjinna for axes," said Billi-billeri, "as our People have many times talked. But so have the Mogullumbitch and the Ballung-Karar before you. The Boi-berrit have come, and the Kurnung-willam and the Kurung-jang-baluk and the Bunurong, the Baluk-willam, and the Waring-illam. The Nirabaluk, the Jajaurung, the Thagunworung and the Buthera-baluk, they have come. Even the Echuca have crossed the mountain and come;

and the Meymet; and the Brabralung, they have all come. We cannot talk so much stone. We can talk no more. We cannot talk with you."

Billi-billeri gave the wolard and the kowir skins to Bungerim, who put them down in front of Murrangurk.

Murrangurk dropped his head and wept.

"Billi-billeri," he said. "The mulla-mullung have dreamed that the poles of bwal are rotting, and, if the Old Man does not have more stone, the sky will fall."

"That dream we have had," said Billi-billeri.

And he sang.

"In the Beginning, when the waters parted, and the Ancestors Dreamed all that is, and woke the life that slept, the sky lay on the earth, and the sun could not move, until the Magpie lifted the sky with a stick."

"A stick!" said the People.

"And when the Dreaming was done, and each Ancestor made of himself churinga, our Ancestor, Bomjinna, who Dreamed all the land of the Wurunjerri-baluk, the Kurnaje-berring, the Boi-berrit, said, 'I shall be a mountain.' "

"A mountain!"

" 'And I shall sleep.' "

"Sleep!"

" 'But, before my sleeping, I shall shit a great shit.' "

"A great shit!"

" 'And, though you may not wake me, you may take my shit as stone for axes.' "

"Axes!"

" 'They will be black and strong with the power of my shit and my Dreaming.' "

"Dreaming!"

" 'And, in my sleep, I shall also shit, and this, too, you may take for axes. But, if you eat into me, you will kill my Dreaming, and I shall shit no more.' "

"No more!"

" 'And the Wurunjerri-baluk, the Kurnaje-berring, the Boi-berrit, too, they will have no Dreaming, and they will die.' "

"Will die!"

"Then Bomjinna became a mountain, and since then he sleeps."

"He sleeps!"

Billi-billeri ended his song. And Murrangurk wept again.

"If at once all the world comes for axes," said Billi-billeri, "they will eat until Bomjinna is no more, and the Wurunjerri-baluk, the Kurnaje-berring, the Boi-berrit are no more, and the land will die in its Dreaming. What will it matter, then, if the sky should fall? Answer my dream."

"I cannot answer," said Murrangurk.

"But be cheerful!" said Billi-billeri. "You come as wordholders of peace and as guests. We shall dance and sleep, and, with the Morning Star, you shall go back with gifts of spears, and you shall be free of this land, to take roots, and berries and all that you may hunt, till you come to your own land again."

So fires were lit for dancing, and the Kurnaje-berring sang and danced, and the best food was given to Murrangurk and Brairnumin, in honour. Then they slept; and, with the Morning Star, Murrangurk set off down the mountain, Brairnumin carrying the rug and the bags of wolard skin and kowir. And Bomjinna was quiet in his Dreaming.

Murrangurk looked at Brairnumin's footprints.

What weight is in your bag?

Brairnumin did not answer.

Murrangurk opened the kowir bag. Inside were lumps of black stone.

I could not let the sky fall, uncle.

You have stolen the honour of the Beingalite and the trust of the Kurnaje-berring. Thief.

Murrangurk kicked Brairnumin, turned him and drove him back up the mountain, beating him with spears and shield, until they came to the fires again. The crowd that met them parted, and they passed through to where Billi-billeri still sat in his shelter. Murrangurk threw the young man to the ground, and set the kowir bag before Billi-billeri. He took out the stones softly and placed them before him.

Murrangurk went to where Brairnumin lay and thrust his spear through the young man's thigh.

"Forgive the shame, Billi-billeri, that we have brought upon you. Take this blood guilt."

"If you had come, and we had talked stone and not agreed," said Billi-billeri, "it would be blood guilt enough. But it was not so. For while I sang to you of Bomjinna, the young man stole against our Dreaming."

"I am his uncle," said Murrangurk. "I led him to be made a man, and am leading him through the ways of his Dreaming."

"Then you have seen that his Dreaming is small, and its ways few," said Billi-billeri. "His step in the Dance is over. All this you have seen."

"How shall I fill the circle of his Dance?" said Murrangurk. "His father and his mother were killed as I was killed. No one knows the place where his spirit first spoke in the womb, or where the birth blood was buried. Where shall his bones sing?"

"His step is finished," said Billi-billeri. "He has no song. Nothing of him may return to the circle of Being. It is done."

"No," said Murrangurk. "There is a mist; but the Dance is not ended, and a song will be sung."

Hold me, uncle, said Brairnumin. With my eyes I see. There is no mist. Hold me, uncle. I am your way. When you next look into me, you will remember. Dance then for me the step that now I may not. But hold me, uncle.

Brairnumin stood, and put his arms out behind him for Murrangurk to take. He bowed his head, and, with the blow of a konnung club, Bungerim smashed his skull.

Murrangurk caught the body as it fell, and cradled it.

"Take him to Morriock," said Billi-billeri. "Let there be no blood between us."

Murrangurk put the body over his shoulder, gave back the spears of the Kurnaje-berring, lifted the wordholder's spear, and went down from Bomjinna.

25

He saw the smoke of the fires, and the smoke of the fires far to the side, long before the round peak of Morriock, covered with the red bones of Neeyangarra, appeared.

Murrangurk walked across the brown grass down towards Moodiwarri Full of Eels, but he did not go to there. He went to the path of fires, from which came the wailing of the women, and sat for the waters to rise. He put down the shield, the spear and the bags, and slid the body from his shoulder onto the grass. He pressed his hands in the liquid of the flesh, and rubbed the grease on his own skin. Then he painted himself red, and made white circles about his eyes.

Nullamboin came along the path to meet him, wearing the same paint, with kowir and plover in his hair; and Murrangurk stood, lifted the body and set it in Nullamboin's outstretched arms. Nullamboin carried the body to the grave, where more fires burned and men waited. The keening women were further back, swinging firesticks to sear themselves.

Nullamboin opened a net of wolard hair and thrust the head into it, and tied the fists together with another. Two men slit the side with flint, rolled the body in a wolard cloak and put it in a tube of marung bark and laid it in the grave, lined with marung. The People were silent. Murrangurk took the wangim from the kowir bag and set them in the grave. Then the men threw in branches of marung, and on top of them marung logs; and Nullamboin spoke. But the

STRANDLOPER

silence was still on Murrangurk, and he did not hear. The men built up the grave with slow care, and the women moved round it in dance and song, but still Murrangurk heard nothing. As the mound began to rise, he left and went to sit where he had first come.

Nullamboin sat by him, and waited.

"Who put the spear through the thigh of a wordholder?"

"I put the spear through him," said Murrangurk, "because he was thief to the Kurnaje-berring and took their stone. It was Billi-billeri who killed."

"Why did Billi-billeri kill a wordholder?"

"There is no blood between us," said Murrangurk.

"How can there not be blood for murder of the sacred?"

"So many wordholders of stone have come," said Murrangurk, "that no more can be talked, for Bomjinna would be eaten, and the Dreaming of the Kurnaje-berring would die."

"It is finished," said Nullamboin. "The sky will fall."

"It is not finished," said Murrangurk. "A thing happened. My nephew died a warrior, and the ways of his Dreaming were short. Yet I have led him through his Dreaming, and his ways were not short. I saw them, uncle. And he, too, saw them, with his eyes, and he spoke true to me, but I cannot tell his meaning."

"The sky will fall, but his ways are not short," said Nullamboin. "Kah!"

"For seven days I have walked," said Murrangurk, "and no answer has come to me."

"Your head is a cloud of grief," said Nullamboin. "Go up onto Morriock to the bones of Neeyangarra, and hear them. And gather coraminga and torumba; nardoo, goborro, mulkathandra, bolwarra; mara, karagata, dargan. And when you have gathered them, and heard the Ancestor, wait."

Nullamboin stood and went to the fires of Moodiwarri Full of Eels. When Purranmurnin Tallarwurnin saw that the men had ended their speaking, she brought the kidney fat of the young man, on a leaf, and Murrangurk took it and ate it and put black paint about his mouth, in honour of his nephew who had died a warrior.

"Come now and rest," she said. "It is finished."

"It is not finished," said Murrangurk. "I must go alone."

He climbed the slope, between the rocks and trees.

In the Beginning, when the waters parted and the Ancestors Dreamed all that is, and woke the life that slept, the sky lay on the earth, and the sun could not move, until the Magpie lifted the sky with a stick.

And when the Dreaming was done, and each Ancestor made of himself churinga, Bunjil had strong poles of bwal set around the sky; and he put the Old Man to look after them and keep them firm, so that the sky should not fall.

Then Bunjil trod upon the whirlwind and rode beyond the Hard Darkness, and he sits in Tharangalkbek to look upon the living and to guide the dead.

The Ancestor Neeyangarra, father of eagles, had the world of songs, and he taught his songs to the eagles that are the flesh of all mulla-mullung; but he did not teach all his songs to every son, nor did every son teach all his songs to every mulla-mullung, nor did every mulla-mullung teach all his songs to the People.

When he had shaped the land and the rivers and the lakes, Neeyangarra made Morriock for his seat, and he listened to the songs; and they woke the cry of everlasting life within him, and he went up as a fire of flame, and his hollow bones covered Morriock, that the wind might blow and the songs be true.

And from the ashes of his feathers grew the marung tree of everlasting life, in the turn of its Dreaming. Its seeds were small, but had the wings of their father and his songs gave them wisdom, and they became Thuroongarong, the bee. And when Bunjil saw this, he gave the bee the voice of Tundun, his own son of ever-lasting life, and taught the bee to take sweetness from the flowers and make the honey of everlasting life for all the People.

And so the red bones of fire lay between the marung trees, and Murrangurk sat on the hill top and wept that now the sky should fall.

He lay at night and looked up at the stars, and thought which was the fire of his nephew on that journey to Tharangalkbek. Then he closed his eyes, and listened to the songs of the wind in the stone, and he slept.

The next day he gathered the branches and the leaves as Nul-lamboin had told, and then he waited.

The water on Morriock was small, and he had no food, but the bees fetched honey to his lips. He looked until he found a white feather of Coonardoo, and, when the bee fed him, he held it gently and stuck the feather on its back and let it go. He followed the white feather of Coonardoo among the trees and over the rocks, until the bee came to its nest. He pulled the feather away, and watched the bees dance.

Murrangurk learned the dance with the sound of the voice of Tundun from their wings. The bees taught him Thuroongarong, and each day he went to the nest and shared the dance of his new flesh.

So he danced, and at night he listened to Neeyangarra's songs, and hunted the fire among the shining bees, whose dance was the turn of marung into the dawn and the Morning Star. Calm came to his grief.

At the height of the day, he saw men on the grass below Morriock.

He went back to his sleeping place, and painted his body red, and yellow, and put four curved lines of white across his chest to show the combs of his Bee flesh. He took kowir and plover from his medi-cine bag, and the feather of an eagle's wing, and fixed them in his headband. He put a koim bone through his nose, and tied bwal about his arms and around his ankles. The black ring at his mouth he left, to remember his nephew and his death for the sky.

Now his spirit was ready. To this he had been born. There was no more that he could do.

Every elder had come, and they sat until the waters had risen, then went to Murrangurk.

Nullamboin gave him a bag of wolard skin, and said, "Here are the ways of your Dreaming. It was for this I sang, and for this I danced."

Murrangurk took the bag and walked. The elders followed in a line.

At the top of Morriock grew a marung tree, and about it bees flew. Murrangurk and the elders sat. They did not speak. They turned their minds towards the tree.

Murrangurk opened the bag, and took out the churingas of his Dreaming. He held each one, and traced the song that was carved into it, from the beginning to the ending. The tips of the churinga were bare, and sacred to the Dream, for its song to grow from the silence that went before, and to make the silence of the greater Dream to come.

All day they sat. And when the light went and the bees flew to their nest, Wolmutang, Tarrupitch, Burkamuk and Karrin stood at the four points of the sky and swung churingas about their heads on ropes, so that the voice of Tundun would not fade. But the rest kept their thoughts upon the tree, and Murrangurk traced his songs again, to hold pure his spirit; and when he had finished he took the coraminga, the torumba, the nardoo, gobboro, mulkathandra, bolwarra, mara, karagata and the dargan that he had gathered, and, within a shelter of spearthrowers, blew a fire heap from them.

Then he waited, putting his thought to the tree.

A wind came, and the branches moved. It was a small wind, but the branches swept forward, and the trunk bent. It bent over and down, until it touched the ground, and it dipped its head in the glowing.

Then the marung of everlasting life sprang upright in one blaze, and was a bird of flame, an eagle that climbed into the air, and his feathers were churingas of fire, and each churinga a burning song.

Neeyangarra grew and spread his wings until the sky was covered; and he stooped to where Murrangurk sat.

Murrangurk lifted to meet him; and, as he came nearer, the eagle shrank, until he was a star, and the star went into Murrangurk at his mouth, and he felt the churingas of flame. There was tearing of beak and claw, his bones were the red rocks and his head a world of song.

26

"Henny-Penny!"

He sat upright, out of sleep.

"Tongue of my heart, what is it?" said Purranmurnin Tallarwurnin, holding him.

"What?"

"You spoke."

"What did I say?"

"They were words of sound, without meaning."

Murrangurk scooped water and drank, then put red on his headband, painted the red lines across his eyes, and nose and cheek bones, the two lines down the middle of his chest, turning along the bottom ribs, the shorter lines that did not turn, and put white dots around them. He drew the solemn path of the snake upon his arms and legs, and marked its fires with a dot in the curve of each bend.

Nullamboin watched from his shelter.

There is a cloud on the sea from Narrm, said Murrangurk. It is at Beangala.

Sing strong, said Nullamboin.

Murrangurk gathered all his weapons: his shield, the spearthrower, his war spears, wangim and barngeet.

"Where are you going?" said Purranmurnin Tallarwurnin.

"To Beangala," said Murrangurk.

"Never as you are shall you return," said Purranmurnin Tallarwurnin.

"How can I hurt you who am myself?" said Murrangurk. "I must go. It is my Dreaming."

He left the fires, across the marshes towards Beangala. An eagle hung above him.

He travelled for a time, until he smelt two men coming towards him. They were young warriors, Pulmadaring and Wolmudging, and they carried their spears high, waving them. At the points hung bright colours. When they saw Murrangurk, they ran to meet him and gave him the spears. The colours were squares, tightly woven, one green, one blue.

"Grandfather," said Pulmadaring, "there are dead men at Beangala, and they are alive!"

"They have made fire," said Wolmudging, "and have eaten koim, without talk, and they will not go, but gave us these. They eat the land, without talk, and give us these! But we are not enough to fight them. Come and tell the People."

"I cannot come," said Murrangurk. "The dead men do not know our way. I shall go to them, and talk peace."

He gave back the spears.

"We have no peace with thieves of the land," said Pulmadaring. "The earth shakes; and the warriors are gathering."

Murrangurk watched them go, then he ran.

He tasted the smoke of a fire, and moved in silence, looking.

Near the shore of Beangala he saw a pole, and from it hung something coloured red, white and blue, but, although he had seen it before, he could not give the thin rug a name. He went nearer. The pole was by a fire, and, around the fire, the men had built a barrier of wood. They were white men. He saw three. And there were five other people, but they were covered with the same stuff, and no paint showed what else they were.

There were shelters of white, and he knew them, too; but again they had no name; and there was a shelter of turf.

Outside the barrier was a hole. He saw a man dip something into it and drink. When the man went back, Murrangurk moved to the hole and sat. He could hear the men talking, and again he knew the sounds, he had known them and spoken them, yet what they meant once had dried on the wind; but he saw dreams that he had forgotten, and smelt fear, and was himself afraid. Murrangurk sat and did not move.

One of the people saw him, and pointed. They all turned and began to talk loudly, and to look around. At last, they became quiet, but watched. And when he felt that the waters had risen, Murrangurk stood, and walked forward.

"Cheese it. What's this fly clapperdodgeon?"

"Gaw! Clap yer glims on that for a bastardly gullion!"

The sounds. He heard them. What were they?

"Joe, you askim he sabby," said a white man to one of the people. When Murrangurk looked into him, he saw that the spirit was broken, and he did not know his tongue, but the man knew what Murrangurk was, and dropped his gaze.

"Boss, him no sabby," said Joe. "Him one bigpela bossman bilong here. Him scare dispela plenty toomuch. Him bigpreest bilong blackpela. Him mabn. Him got song, him got eye, bilong kill."

The white man stood in front of Murrangurk and smiled. He gestured, and spoke in a shout.

"Do! Be! Seated! My friend!"

Murrangurk looked at him.

"Please! Sit! Here!" And the man sat on the ground and patted it with his hand.

Murrangurk understood. He sat next to the man, but he kept his weapons across his lap. He looked into the man. The man was kind. He meant no harm. Why did he shout? Why did he not know silence?

Why could he not feel death coming? Murrangurk must tell him, but how could he? The man's mind was filled with noise.

"Pray! Take! Food!"

He held a lump of brown moss and put it into Murrangurk's hand. Murrangurk smelt it.

Coloured dreams came back and joined each other. Not everything. But enough. His tongue and ears opened, and he spoke.

"Bread."

"What?" The man's mouth was loose, his eyes wide.

"Bake – Break – Bread. 'A slice off a cut loaf isn't missed.' "

One of the other men pulled Murrangurk's hair and beard aside.

"He's no chimneychops! The cove's bug!"

They sprang away from him. Murrangurk was on his feet in a move, shield and spear poised.

"Don't – send – back – "

"Send? Where?" said the first man.

"Pris – on – " said Murrangurk.

"There's no clink from here to Port Jackson," said the other.

"No. Yes. Sull-ivan Bay."

"Sullivan Bay? Not for thirty years and more, friend. The colony failed."

"Thirty? Years? Thirty? Three? Ten? Ten? Ten?"

"Put down your spear, old man. No one will hurt you."

"Will – . William. William Buck-ley?"

"Cut bene! What's these inching cuffins?"

A war party came from between the trees. It appeared as if out of the ground. Murrangurk fell between the worlds, and dropped his weapons, and lay on his face.

"Shoot! Shoot!"

"There's fifty and more. We've no chance."

The warriors began to grunt, and they clashed their spears on their

[164]

shields. The sound spoke to Murrangurk. He got up, and, unarmed, went beyond the barrier. The warriors were still.

Murrangurk took the thundal from his medicine bag and held it up so that it flashed rainbows, and the warriors gasped and hid their eyes with their shields.

Murrangurk sang.

"I of the Kal Dreaming! Flesh of Thuroongarong! Son of Nee-yangarra! Son of Binbeal, son of Mami-ngata, with his eagle!" He pointed above, and the warriors saw where the eagle hung. "And I have been dead before. But it is you who will die now. Though you may kill these, and though you kill many, yet more will come. Their featherfoot men are more than the stars of the sky. And if you kill even them, more will come, without end. They are more than the stars of the sky. They are more than the sand of the sea. Go. If you do not kill these men, they will bring gifts for you all, and for the women and for the elders, and will talk koim and all other trouble. It is I, Murrangurk, that sing!"

The warriors shuffled their feet and looked at the ground. They turned, and were gone.

Murrangurk came back inside the barrier and sat.

"Safe now," he said.

"Can you be sure?"

"With your people, I am a little man," said Murrangurk. "With my People, I sing strong. Safe now. But not prison. Not prison."

"It's a King's Pardon for you, my matey, if William Todd has a word in it," said the white man.

"Bread," said Murrangurk. "Grand as owt."

27

Every day, Murrangurk waited for the cloud of sail to appear on the horizon.

He had been left with two of the white men and their People until the ship arrived. He went back to his own fires, and moved the women and the warriors to the Place of Growing, for safety, and returned to Beangala with Nullamboin and most of the elders. They made their shelters next to the white men, and Murrangurk stayed with them.

The cloud came. Murrangurk watched. The ship hit a sandbank some way from the shore, and a boat was lowered. Then a cannon fired, and Murrangurk felt the claws of Neeyangarra within him, in joy and pain, for William Todd had said that, if he came back with the pardon, the cannon would be the sign.

The boat was drawn up on the shore and William Todd stepped out, smiling, and holding a parchment fastened with red silk. He gave it to Murrangurk.

"This is for you, Will."

"Is it me pardon?"

"Open it."

Murrangurk broke the seal, untied the ribbon and unrolled the parchment.

"From the Governor," he said.

"You could look more pleased."

"There's promises," said Murrangurk.

"Then keep them."

"How can I?"

"I have secured you preferment and a situation."

"What's that?"

"Your adventures are all the talk, and I have found a decent man who will provide you with food and drink, clothing and lodging, and remuneration besides."

"What should I want with them?"

"But you cannot enter society as you are."

"And what makes this gentleman so kind as to do all this for the likes of me?"

"He keeps a tavern and a music hall. It is his plan to show your marvellous adventures in a public spectacle, a divertissement: how you overcome the might of the militia in Man's universal struggle to be free; how you brave the savages, through Almighty Providence, in your wanderings in the wilderness, and subdue their brutish natures to God's wisdom in making you their king; and how, in the end, by your steadfastness to Him who shed His blood for all men, you are purged of Sin. For this, my friend will pay you eleven pounds per annum, all found. Will this not aid your promises, if, as I suspect, you mean your passage home, which could be yours in but a few years' time?"

"You've been right good to me," said Murrangurk.

"There would have been none to thank, without Will Buckley. Is that not so, Mr Batman?"

There was another white man in the boat. He had eyes that did not move when he looked at Murrangurk. Murrangurk saw that he would not speak the truth.

"What is it you're at, coming here?" said Murrangurk.

"To settle the land and to run sheep," said Batman. "The first flocks are with us."

"And what shall you eat while you're at this caper?" said Murrangurk.

"There is game, and we have sown crops," said Batman.

"And what's us lot supposed to do?" said Murrangurk, nodding towards the elders.

"The niggers shall move," said Batman. "They are few, the country is large, and there is room for all. And we cannot have them worrying the sheep."

"If you try at shifting us," said Murrangurk, "you'll happen find more nor what you bargained for. 'Empty bellies don't have ears,' think on. I'm telling you. It's here as we belong."

"Here. Elsewhere. What does it matter?" said Batman.

"Matter? I'll tell you what it matters," said Murrangurk. "If we're shifted, we'll not thole. And if we don't thole, land dies. It needs walking, and it's us must walk it. Do you not see? We're all one, and have been since I don't know when, since Beginning. It's same as, like, whatsitsname, what-d'ye-call-em. Church! Yay! If you flit any on us, we'll not live; and just you see: neither will land. We must have each other – "

"This is sentimental nonsense."

" – same as Mami-ngata said! Same as Bible!"

"The man's deranged and blasphemous."

" 'For all the land which thou seest, to thee will I give it, and to thy seed for ever.' Look ye! I remember me Bible! So you just bugger off back where you come from!"

"But here you are wrong, Buckley. Read me this."

Batman spread out a sheet of parchment, ornately written. Murrangurk peered at it.

" 'Know all Persons that We Three Brothers, Jagajaga, Jagajaga, Jagajaga, being the Principle Chiefs' – Nay! You read it! 'Jagajaga'? What's all this nominy? 'Jagajaga'? So's me arse! Chiefs? Give over!

And we don't write us names in pen and ink, neither!"

"Nevertheless," said Batman, "this document shows and proves that I have bought one hundred thousand acres of this land for twenty pair of blankets, thirty knives, twelve tomahawks, ten looking glasses, twelve pair scissors, fifty handkerchiefs, twelve red shirts, four flannel jackets, four suits of clothes and fifty pounds of flour. The land is mine. I own it."

"Nay, youth," said Murrangurk. "The land owns us: every mortal one. But you! My song! Coming here! You've pissed chalice and shitten church!"

Murrangurk walked away and sat at the fire with the elders.

"The creature could threaten our venture," said Batman. "We must remove him."

"But, sir, he has prevented massacre," said William Todd. "We are greatly indebted to him. And the people hold him in high repute. It would be a madness to meddle with him."

"Allow me credit for a little wit, friend Todd," said Batman. "Without his good offices, we should indeed be at risk. No. His fortune must become our special care."

"But there will be war among all the nations," said Derrimut. "Then the Mogullumbitch will kill the Ballung-Karar, the Ballung-Karar the Wurunjerri-baluk, the Wurunjerri-baluk the Bunurong, the Bunurong the Kurung, the Kurung the Beingalite, we the Kaurn-kopan, they the Gournditch-Mara, and so to the end of the world. Where are my spears? I shall make him peace!"

"It is of no use, cousin," said Murrangurk. "He speaks as one I dreamed once, who cared for nothing but his wish, felt no honour to the laws of elders, nor thought for any but his own. We cannot move these men. They will not go. They will swallow the world. Now my Dreaming truly begins. For this Nullamboin sang, and for this he danced."

"For this you are one with Neeyangarra," said Nullamboin. "For this you have his songs. So, too, did I sing and dream, long ago, that you might come. Now is your Dreaming, now your song."

"Buckley. A word with you." Batman spoke. Murrangurk got up from the fire and went to him.

"Buckley. I have been thinking. Although my claim to this land is beyond dispute, I must own that communication with the natives, and their understanding of my claim, are matters of some difficulty. Could we not strike a bargain? If you were to accompany me for some months as translator, since I believe you are conversant with their several tongues, and if you were to lend your undoubted authority to my dealings with the chiefs, I should be prepared, at our conclusion, to fund your passage to England. What do you say to that?"

Murrangurk looked up. The eagle was above him.

"Ay. Fair do's."

He looked again. The eagle was still there.

28

"I am glad to see you, Murrangurk, but you must be gentle and hurt no one and speak straight."

Billi-billeri smoothed the ground with his hand. Murrangurk sat. He was painted white, marked with black.

"I am glad to see you, Billi-billeri," he said, "and I have come with these men who are dead, to talk land and to talk trees."

I have come to hold the Dreaming and to make it new, said his paint.

"How are we to talk land and trees, when they are not ours to talk?" said Billi-billeri. The dead men shall die again, said his arm.

"They bring gifts," said Murrangurk. Do not kill them, said his shoulders. Many must die, and you will die, whatever you may wish. It cannot be stopped. But if you kill now, all will die. These men have come to take the land. They swallow the world. I am here so that others may find their ways in the Dreaming.

"We thank them for their gifts, and will talk," said Billi-billeri. What shall we do with our spirit? said his fingers. Our piece of Time is not used, our step not ended. Where shall we walk?

"That is good," said Murrangurk. I was sung to bring a new Time, a new Dreaming, said his hands, and in them you yourself shall walk. My Ancestor, Neeyangarra, speaks this.

"Then let us eat," said Billi-billeri, "and sing, and dance upon the earth." He smiled at the white men.

"Does he agree?" said Batman.

"Ay," said Murrangurk. "Soft as Dick's hatband. You've getten more than you bargained for here."

"Good fellow," said Batman. "That is the way to do it."

"I hope your bums are tough," said Murrangurk. "You'll be sitting all night with this lot."

They gave knives and axes when they left in the morning. For Billi-billeri there was a looking glass, and he smiled into it again.

"Vanity is a cheap currency, Heaven be praised," said Batman to Todd as they rode down from Bomjinna.

"And no error," said Murrangurk, who walked beside them. "Who's next?"

They went from the Kurnaje-berring to the Boi-berrit, the Wurun-jerri-baluk, the Ngaruk-willam, the Balak-willam, the Ediboligit-oorong, the Yalukit and all the Bunurong, and, after the talking and the journeying, to the settlement on the Birrarrung at Narrm.

Well, that's reckoned him up, said Murrangurk. Rump and stump, it has. Ay. Rump and stump.

Batman and Todd had to be lifted from their horses, and they were put into bath tubs and washed by their servants, Pigeon and Bill Bullets, of the Camaraigal, of Port Jackson, who were waiting for them.

"When's me ship?" said Murrangurk.

"There will be one next month," said Batman. "I suggest that you spend some of that period in restoring yourself to the likeness of a civilised being."

"Time enough for that," said Murrangurk. "I'm just off for a stroll, me. I'll be back in a threeweek." He marked his arm with bands for each day. "Be good, and then." He set off along the beach.

By, this here wants some walking. It always did.

He kept on the move, staying at the water. It was Bunurong land, and though there was no quarrel between them and the Beingalite when he had left, the Bunurong were never trusted. Yet, he walked the shore for them, and danced the Morning Star, and sang their songs at any Place of Growing that he saw. But he made no fires, and drank from no roots, took none of their food, and slept lightly beneath his eagle.

He was glad to cross the river into his own land, to see the peaks of the Youangs, where the bee thunder had spoken to him and given him its drink.

Now he built a fire, and hunted. And he stayed a while, feeling the strength of the land under his feet, and dancing the strength back to the land each night.

He reached Kooraioo, and was near Woodela, when he saw that there were too many crows ahead. He stopped, and climbed a tree. The crows were feeding in scattered groups. He smelt meat.

Murrangurk waited in the tree, but nothing else was moving, so he came down and went inland towards the crows. There was a straight line of fencing not honouring the land. He sat by it, but there were only the crows and the meat. No one had passed that day, and there was no smoke. He went forwards across the grass, and the nearest crows called out to him to stay away, but when they thought that he did not understand, they turned back to their feeding until he was so close that they grumbled and flew up. He looked at his eagle. It had risen high to avoid the pack.

Murrangurk stood above the dead animal. It was a sheep. The crows had taken the soft parts first and were working the insides. They had just begun on the meat under the wool, and so Murrangurk could see the spear hole above the heart. But none had been taken by the hunter.

It was the same wherever he went. Young and old, tups, ewes and lambs, had all been killed and left. There were more than he could count.

Murrangurk walked among the corpses across the plain, and every crow warned him not to go further, yet he had to. In front of him the plain became a low ridge, and beyond that he smelt another, and a different, death.

He stood on the ridge. The land fell away towards the Place of Growing. There were more bodies of sheep, but from the branches of every tree hung men, tied by their hair, and no crows were on them.

Murrangurk painted his face white before he went to the trees. He looked up at the first man. They were all warriors of the Beingalite, and they had been shot. He saw his nephews and his grandsons and his sons, the young men whose Dreamings he had led, whose ways he had taught, the young men he had held at their Smoking. But it was not their bodies he saw, but their skins only. The meat and bones had been taken out, and grass had been stuffed into them. It hung from their eyes, their noses, their mouths, and all around him Murrangurk heard the cry of their trapped spirits. There was an elder among them. It was Derrimut.

Murrangurk climbed each tree and untied the hair, and, gentle, lowered the skin to the ground. Then he gathered them, as many as he could lift, and carried them to the Place of Growing and piled them between the Clashing Rock and the water of the Spirit Hole, and went back to bring more; back and forth, until all were together. Then he took a wangim and went to where the crows were feeding, and he killed a crow, for the Beingalite were of the Crow flesh. He put the bones of the crow with the skins of the warriors, to be the bones of them all.

He danced the Crow, and he danced the Evening Star, which calls the warriors home. Then he blew a fire heap, and put it to the skins; and while they burned he sat and sang to them. He sang of the Beginning, of the Ancestors, and their Dreaming of all that was and is; he sang to lift them to the sky for the track to Tharangalkbek, and the songs of Life and of Death that had come to him from Neeyangarra he sang also. And when he had sung, Murrangurk danced the strength that had been theirs back to the earth, so that it would not go with them. He danced until bone and skin were dust; then he took the dust and spread it on the water of the Spirit Hole, and the warriors were put back into the circle of Being to begin the new step of their Dance. So all was done.

Murrangurk picked up his shield and his weapons and walked in the purple light and the rising moon to where the fires of the People were.

They came out to meet him: Nullamboin, Koronn his wife and Purranmurnin Tallarwurnin. They sat, facing him, and Murrangurk howled, and tore at the grass and flung earth over himself and fell backwards as if dead.

The others went to him and raised him. He stood, and they held him and set him by the fires, and Purranmurnin Tallarwurnin brought him water to drink, and cleansed his body and his spirit with leaves of bwal, and sang him back to her.

"What has happened?" said Murrangurk, looking at them. "Why are you so horrible to see?"

Nullamboin was dressed as a white man. He wore a hat, a shirt, flannel jacket and breeches. Koronn wore a dress of dyed cotton, and Purranmurnin Tallarwurnin a dress striped green and blue.

"They say that we are animals," said Nullamboin, "and will not feed us. They make us put on these things that hurt."

"Kah!" said Murrangurk.

"The animals with white hair kill all the land. The dead men say that they must have the land. They will not let the warriors hunt."

"The dead men will not let the women gather roots and berries and the small meat," said Koronn. "There are only children and elders now."

"Where are the young women and their Dreaming?" said Murrangurk.

"The dead men take them," said Koronn. "And when they have finished, they kill them, or cut their teats and turn them loose."

Nullamboin stood. He took off his hat and threw it onto the fire and put kowir and plover in his hair. He painted his face red, and white and black. The elders gathered. "I sing," said Nullamboin; "for it is a time to die."

And Nullamboin sang.

"There is a mulla-mullung. He is white and he is mad. I look into him and see no Ancestor, no Mami-ngata; nothing is his flesh, he has no Dreaming."

"No Dreaming!"

"He talks to the air, and says it is a spirit. I see no spirit."

"No spirit!"

"He says the spirit will feed us if we say that it is good and that we are bad."

"Are bad!"

"He says that, if we do not, the spirit will be angry and will hold firesticks against our skins for ever."

"For ever!"

"He says that we must eat the spirit. We must not blacken our mouths."

"Our mouths!"

"He does not blacken his mouth; but he says that what he drinks is its blood."

"Its blood!"

"He says that it gives him power."

"Him power!"

[176]

"He says that, when he does wrong, and drinks the blood, he is forgiven; and when he does wrong again, he drinks again."

"Drinks again!"

"And, if he drinks, he will live for ever."

"For ever!"

"Now an elder, Kal cousin of Murrangurk, dreams to be mulla-mullung. He dreams to take this power and to live for ever; and he finds the blood of the spirit in a bowl."

"A bowl!"

"A round bowl of black flint, closed with wood: so. And the elder takes the bowl, and drinks; and he is mad."

"Is mad!"

"He gives the blood to the warriors, to them all; and all are mad."

"Are mad!"

"They make war on the animals that eat the land, and kill them."

"Kill them!"

"But the blood that they drink does not save them, and the dead men kill the warriors and the elder, and will not let us take them to their places of birth blood."

"Birth blood!"

"They steal the skin from them and hang it on trees, and the bones and meat they give to kal."

"To kal!"

"I hear the warriors weeping."

"Weeping!"

"Now the Beingalite will pass. For we are elders, and shall be gone before the children can be led into the ways of their Dreaming. The sky has fallen. My song has ended. The Dance is dead."

29

Murrangurk danced the Morning Star.

"Why do you dance?" said Nullamboin. "Have you not heard me?"

"Why do you ask?" said Murrangurk. " 'The grass of your head is white.' "

Nullamboin laughed. "But yours is the whiter."

They sat by the fire.

"My song was poor last night."

"New songs must be sung until they are smooth," said Murrangurk. "And it is hard for a man to sing when his balls are not loose."

"Kah," said Nullamboin.

"But you did sing strong when you sang me. Now it is my singing."

"There is a dream that I have not told you," said Nullamboin. "It was the dream before I sang, so long ago. You dance in a forest of brown wood. Your step is with the voice of Tundun. You dance into silence. The silence and the song are all and one. What does it mean?"

"It sings true," said Murrangurk. "It is the dream of a warrior."

"We are warriors," said Nullamboin. "I tell you this. The dead men kill us, take our bodies, take the land. Now they would take the sacred; but we fight. They will build fires in the place beyond Kooraioo. They will be big fires that will not move. And they build them so that more and more and more of their animals can come; and they ask me the name of the place beyond Kooraioo, so that the people with broken spirit who serve them will know where to come. We cannot save the place beyond Kooraioo, but we can send its name into the Dreaming. 'What name, old man,' say the dead men, 'is it called, so that the people may know it?' I think swift. 'Its name,' I say to them, 'is Pissflaps.' 'Pissflaps,' say the dead men. 'It will be a mighty fire for ever.' "

Nullamboin and Murrangurk cried with laughter.

"Oh, uncle, you sing strong! Dead men cannot win!"

They stood. Murrangurk looked into Nullamboin. Nullamboin welcomed him.

> Owd Cob and Young Cob
> And Young Cob's son;
> Young Cob's Owd Cob
> When Owd Cob's done.

Nullamboin knew.

Now I must sing, said Murrangurk. They grasped the shoulders and spoke into the eyes. Dance well. They shall not take the Dreaming.

Murrangurk turned, and walked away, and did not look back.

"Pissflaps!" shouted Nullamboin.

"Pissflaps, uncle!"

He went to his fire and held Purranmurnin Tallarwurnin's hands, and held them. The bones were quiet, the bones of a bird.

They sat, and remembered.

Go now, she said. We are one Dreaming.

We are one Dreaming.

He left, and did not look back.

Murrangurk went to the grave with the two trees. The bark had covered the edges of the spirit lines cut into the wood, but he read their ways.

At the Place of Growing, he painted his body red and yellow, and put four curved lines of white across his chest to show the combs of his Bee flesh. He took kowir and plover and the feather of an eagle's wing, painted his headband yellow, and across it, in red, the solemn path of the snake, and marked its fires with a dot in the curve of each bend, and set the feathers there. He put a koim bone through his nose in place of a reed, and tied bwal about his arms and around his ankles. Then he sat in turn before the Clashing Rock and before the Tree, and sang them into him. He faced the Spirit Hole.

First he danced the Kal, and then the Crow. He danced the Kowir. He danced Thuroongarong. Then he danced the Eagle. And then he sang again.

He sang his Dreaming, and he sang the songs of Neeyangarra, to the clap of wangim, he sang all the songs of Neeyangarra, which had never been sung; and he sang the feathers of the Eagle onto his arms. He sang the solemn way of the Snake, and then he sang the Rainbow.

The waters of the Spirit Hole bubbled, and Murrangurk sang harder and clapped faster, until he sang songs he did not know that came to him from the waters; and out of the Spirit Hole was the plumed head of Binbeal, the Rainbow, and it lifted into the sky, drawing the body upwards, and arched over and down upon Murrangurk, who rose on his eagle feathers to meet him; and Binbeal opened his mouth and swallowed.

Murrangurk flew into the throat. It was not dark, but full of yellow stars, the Five Points of Time, and their lines made the five sides of the comb of Thuroongarong at the heart; and light, and all around him the veins were the pattern of his spirit upon the trees, and they began to turn about him, and to change.

They straightened into lines that were the net of the burying of the head, the track of Death and Life, and then they moved and were the four-pointed heads of the children of Binbeal who had carried Murrangurk inside the Tree. The heads joined, to four-sided Dreamings, and, in the middle of each, though still a net, were the flowers of coraminga, and torumba; nardoo, goborro, mulkathandra, bolwarra; mara, karagata, dargan and other flowers that he knew but could not name.

Bees fed from the flowers, and took their sweetness to everlasting life, and their wings were the voice of Tundun.

Murrangurk flew the gullet of Binbeal, and the lines of Dreaming were the joined combs of Thuroongarong, and then on to the Six Points of Time, joined as combs; and bees fed.

The flowers and the wings faded, but the voice remained. Murrangurk was carried through the turning rainbow. Ahead of him the way led into the paths of a churinga of crystal; and he traced its paths, and each path brought him knowledge, to the great spiral at its centre. He was carried round and in, until, at the end, was the circle of Being, and into this he sank, and through it, to the Ninth Point of Time, beyond where there is no other known among the People.

He was in the sky, under the stars, and before him, on a block of crystal, Bunjil sat, his white beard flowing over him, and, on each shoulder, a thundal went up to the sky, and Murrangurk could not see their end.

Grandfather, said Murrangurk. I have come to take the Dreaming to where it may be safe and not die.

I know why you have come, said Bunjil. You shall take the Dreaming, and the Dreaming of All. But first you shall take a new name; for your song is almost sung, but your next Dreaming is new. Your Dreaming is ever to walk the boundaries, to be the master of them, and to guide the Dreaming in all Time. For that you must have a new name that none may speak. And it is this.

Bunjil gave Murrangurk a name beyond thought.

Yes, Grandfather.

The Dreaming shall not die, and it shall not be disgraced, said Bunjil. I take it from what is Now; and those who live there only will not know it and will think it dead. And you shall take it to where your step in the Dance began, and there you shall leave the Dreaming. For it is yours to take, but not to sing. That is your way. The Dreaming will wait until another singer comes, because of you, and he will travel as you have travelled, but he will sing in another Time.

And you, who have travelled far, shall travel further, to the churinga of your new Dreaming, your new Time, your new Song.

If that is my way, that is my way, said Murrangurk.

It was not by chance that you were sung, for chance is but a little dream, said Bunjil. We are the bees of the invisible. We gather the honey of the invisible and store it in the great, yellow hive of the visible, for everlasting life.

Take the Dreaming.

Bunjil held out to Murrangurk a crystal.

It is the Murrawun, the father of spearthrowers!

And it is the Dreaming, said Bunjil.

Murrangurk reached out and took the crystal; and fell into light.

He was beside the Spirit Hole. The feathers of his arms lay around him. He held a bag of wolard skin. He opened it, and saw what was inside.

It was a wooden spearthrower, with its peg fixed in gum. Around the neck of the handle was bound string of wolard hair. And all was painted red, with three bands of white above, and three below, the neck and four above the peg. It was a spearthrower of reckoning, used by the featherfoot men alone.

Murrangurk laughed with Bunjil, and their laughter filled Earth and Time. "Oh, Pissflaps!"

V

STRANDLOPER

We all go to the bones
all of them shining white in this Dulur country.
The noise of our father Bunjil
rushing down singing in this heart of mine

Berak.

30

Niggy Bower was on the turnpike.

"Now then, Bricky. It's been a while."

"Yay, but it has," said William.

"How art? And how've you bin?" said Niggy.

"Oh, all agait a-going, tha knows," said William.

"Anyroad, it's good to see thee," said Niggy.

"And thee," said William. "Where shall I find Het?"

"She went living Chorley way," said Niggy. "Up th' Hough."

"Whatever for?"

"Beggars can't be choosers. Be good, youth."

"Be good, Niggy."

He had to get to the oak. He put his face against the bark and looked up at the too brilliant leaves. But he heard its song, and was comforted. He went to the Hamestan and ran his fingers along the smoothed top. The tree and the rock were the same. He went to drink at the mere.

The mere. Where was it? He was staring at a hollow field.

"Hey!"

Niggy was across the field, on the turnpike.

"What's up, Bricky?"

"Where's mere?"

"Mere? It inner! That's where! We drained yon, years back! For taters!"

"You daft sods! You've buggered Spirit Hole!"

"Oh, ay? Be seeing you, Bricky!"

[185]

Niggy went his way. William turned back up the lane. A lurcher came out of the hedge and walked at his heel.

Now then, Gyp.

He came to the farm, and stopped at the gate. He could smell many bodies, and, from inside, he heard a chanting. He listened.

"B. Better is solid virtue than riches in learning."

Tap.

"D. Determination overcomes great difficulties."

Tap.

"K. Kindly excuse the shortcomings of others."

Tap. It was the signal that featherfoot men were passing by, but the voices were the voices of children.

"M. Make use of time to secure eternal happiness."

Tap.

"O. Overcome your passions and evil inclinations."

Tap.

"P. Prayer calms the mind and strengthens the soul."

Tap.

William opened the door. There were ten children sitting on forms in the kitchen, with slates and pencils on their knees. They were facing a blackboard where the sideboard used to be, with lines of writing on it. A man stood with a stick in his hand. A desk was in the place of Grandad's chair by the fire, which was as William remembered it, but the fire was not lit.

The man looked William up and down.

"Yes, my good fellow? May I be of assistance?"

The man could not have led warriors.

"I was living here," said William. "As a lad. That's all. When it were a farm."

"Then your name is Buckley!"

"Ay. William."

"Well, Buckley," said the man, "we are now a school, as you may observe; and at our handwriting and reading practice."

"Can I watch?" said William.

"The vicar is coming to hear our progress," said the man. "But you may stay until he arrives."

The man rapped the blackboard with his stick.

"Now! Together for the gentleman. Q."

"Q. Quietly bear your little daily annoyances."

Tap.

"U. Undervalue not your present advantages."

Tap. The redwhite featherfoot men are near. Everybody hush. No one look. No one see.

William heard a horse in the lane. Outside, the dog growled. Shurrup, Gyp. The growling stopped.

A man dismounted, the door opened, and Edward Stanley came into the room. The children stood.

"Good morning, children," said Edward.

"Good morning, Mr Stanley, sir," the chorus replied.

"Good morning, Mr Woodhead."

"Good morning, Mr Edward," said the schoolmaster. "Be seated, children. We have a visitor, Mr Edward, who is this moment leaving. One Buckley."

"Buckley?" Edward looked around. "Will? Will!"

Edward grasped William by the shoulders, without permission, but William saw that he did not know, and let himself be held.

"Ay, Yedart."

"You have returned!"

"Seemingly."

"From the Antipodes?"

"Well, it was a fair old walk, wherever it was. But it's no more nor I said."

"You shall sup at the vicarage," said Edward. "And we shall talk of Anthropophagi, and of the oceans, and of the men who hold their heads between their shoulders!"

"Shall we?" said William. "Ay, we could." He laughed. "I could sing you me little song for me supper. I could that. And maybe it'd be you as'd do the hand practice. In your little pocket book. What?"

"Forgive me, Mr Woodhead," said Edward. "You must excuse us. My friend and I have much to discuss."

"By all means, Mr Edward," said the schoolmaster.

Edward and William left the school. They stood by Edward's horse.

"Is it you, in truth, Will?"

"Well, I don't know what bugger else," said William. "Now then. So you've getten them at the writing at last."

"I have. I have."

"But isn't it a bit of a way," said William, "from as how I seem to recollect: 'The strongest poison ever known came from Caesar's laurel crown.'? And 'Ancient abuses are not by their antiquity converted into virtues.'?"

"Tyranny holds fast, Will."

"Same as griffin."

"At least I have tried."

"Yay," said William. "But 'It's an ill brid bedeets its own nest.'"

The two men went together up the road, Edward leading his horse.

"How is it that you have come back home?"

"King's Pardon," said William.

"And how did you spend your time in New Holland?"

"Oh, walking, mostly."

"But were there not savages?"

"There were savages, ay; you could say that."

"And are they not cannibal?"

"Now just what do you mean by yon?"

"Do they not devour people?"

"Bits," said William. "When it matters. And what have you been at, Yedart?"

"Minding my flock."

"Right place for 'em."

"And I have studied birds, and have written a book concerning their ways, which has been well received."

"Me, too," said William. "But 'Better fed nor taught!' "

"Will," said Edward, "I owe you an apology for which there is no forgiveness."

"And what's that?" said William.

"The sin of my father against you. And my sin for allowing it."

"Give over," said William. "He were an old nowt, and you a mardy. It couldn't be helped. Besides, it was his step in the Dance. And yours."

"What dance?" said Edward.

"Oh, leave off," said William. "It'd take too long. Just say as it's water down a ditch."

They came to the vicarage.

"I'll not stop," said William. "Not now. But I've fetched summat for thee, Yedart."

He reached into the skin bag that he was carrying and took out what was in it.

"You're to have this, Yedart, and you're to keep it safe, think on. Don't you lose it. You can shove it on the wall, or do what you like, but see as you look after it."

Edward held it in his hands.

"What is it?"

"It's what we use for chucking spears," said William. "You set the end of your spear on this peg, and hold it at the handle. Then you flirt it over and forrard, and doesn't it give some thrutch! It does that!"

"An extraordinary and ingenious mechanical device indeed," said Edward. "And could you use it?"

"I could and all."

"When you were accompanying the savages," said Edward, "what was your appellation, your name?"

He felt for his pocket book. William looked at it.

"That's for thee to ask and me to know," said William. "They're very particular about names, are savages."

"Do their names have any significance?"

"I'll say so!"

"Can you tell me what yours signified?"

"Yon's a bit of a poser. You see, I've getten a new un. It says what I do."

"And what is it that you do?" said Edward. His pencil was in one hand, the pocket book in the other, the spearthrower under his arm.

"Well: I'm sort of like a governor, making folks shape," said William; "crossing back and to; there's always summat wants fettling; and same as Grandfather says: 'As good be an addled egg as an idle brid.' So I'm never still, me."

"You could be describing an esturine plover," said Edward: "a most busy creature. Its common name is strandloper, in the southern hemisphere. Aegialitis tricollaris."

"That's the twang. Non omnis moriar. Yay," said William. "Strandloper. She'll do."

"Extraordinary," said Edward. He fumbled and turned the piece of wood in his hand. "To have arrived at this could not have been the act of empiricism. It implies a capacity for abstract thought found among superior beings alone. But what is the purpose of its colouring?"

"Ah. That's what you're to look after it for," said William. "Yon's not just any old stick. It's special. It's used by what we call featherfoot men."

"Featherfoot?"

"They're a bit like parish constable, but with more to 'em. You see, if anyone kills a feller with spells, or some such, the featherfoots go after him with this; and that's him done for, clean as nip."

"They kill others, in belief of magic?" said Edward.

"Sarn it, youth," said William. "A feller's dead, anyroad. Now then. You take a pendulum on a clock. If it swings too far, it has to be put right, else we'd not know where we were, should us? Same with everything. Same with folks, beasts, moon, sun and stars. They've all got to be reckoned. Now what's yon as catches pendulum, and sends it back?"

"The escapement?"

"That's your man," said William. "Escapement. It stops clock to make it right, doesn't it? Stop. Start. Back and to for evermore. You'd not have time without you'd escapement. Well, that's what featherfoots are for. So you look after yon. It's the escapement."

"Why do you require this of me?" said Edward.

"All along of because," said William.

"Because of what?" said Edward.

"Because, though you're a lean dog for a hard road, Yedart," said William, "and one to make a sick man sorrow and a dead man woe, you've a velvet true heart. And you're Brid and Babby flesh, same as me."

"Oh, my friend," said Edward, "I fear that your wanderings in such a clime, and your exposure to the savages, have undermined your intellect."

"You know what's up with you lot," said William. "You've getten one dream less and one skin more."

He walked on, and did not look back.

~~~~~~~~~

31

He followed the turnpike through Sitherton, past Redesmere and over Monks' Heath, by Radnor Wood, and took the path up the long ridge back by White Barn to the top, where it flattened out at Mount Ship and Castle Rock. He sat on the brim of the rock and looked down the four hundred feet to the fields and the house below.

He was thirsty. A lizard crawled from under a stone to bask, and he grabbed it, knocked its head, and opened its skin with his teeth. The meat was sweet, and the juices cooled him. He walked along the ridge until he could climb down among the trees and into Holy Well Slack by Glaze Hill to the house. He sat at the hedge cop of the garden and waited for the waters to rise.

There was a low room at the end of the house, and in it he heard a rattle, and sound like clapsticks, but it was no dance that he knew.

Esther came out of the back door of the house and went into the garden to a stone slab. He watched her, but did not speak.

She was wearing a straw hat with a wide brim, and from it hung a black veil. She had on a dark dress, with a high neck, and the veil tucked into the neck. The wrists and bodice were tight. She had on a white pinafore, and strung drawers were tucked into her boots. Her hands were gloved, and she carried a pail of water. She saw him.

" 'Oh, can you wash a soldier's shirt?' " sang William.

" 'And can you wash it clean?' " she answered.

" 'Oh, can you wash a soldier's shirt – ' "

" 'And hang it on the green?' Now then, Will."

"Now then, Het."

"That's a rum way of sitting. You'll do yourself a mischief, I shouldn't wonder. Where have you been this journey?"

"Oh, 'up atop of down yonder, miles-endy-way, tha knows, at Bog of Mirollies where cats kittlen magpies.'"

She laughed.

"And what are you at?" he said.

"Just taking a skep of honey."

"You're never going to drown them bees!"

"Yay, but I am. How else?"

"You munner kill them. They've getten spirit same as thee."

He stood up and went to her. The dog lay on the cop. "Hold still," William said to Esther, and he started to dance the Bee. Esther dropped the pail and ran to the door. He danced Thuroongarong.

"Will?"

He danced.

"Is that what they learn you?"

He danced. And stopped. He lifted the skep from the stone and turned it. Esther slammed the door shut, and then opened it a crack.

"Will! You're daft! They'll have you!"

William began to sing. And the bees left the skep and settled on him, over him, his clothes and face and skin, until no part of him could be seen but the burs of their hair and wings. And he sang.

When the skep was empty he took out a comb of honey. He looked at it. The comb was a Dreaming, but flat at the tip where it had been fixed to the skep. There was no silence for a greater Dream. Yet the net of the comb was the Six Points of Time, the Joining of the Song.

He took out all the combs and laid them on the slab. The bees left him and flew back to the skep. He put it down, and picked up the combs. Esther opened the door.

"Well, they do learn you summat," she said.

[193]

"Ay. They do," said William.

"Come thi ways within air of the fire, and get some warmship."

She led him into the house. He had to stoop beneath the beams. "Sit thee down. Tek thi bacca. Stick thi nose up chimney."

He put the combs on the slopstone she had covered with white linen and sat on the floor by the hearth.

"You're looking well."

"Ay."

"Shall you have a wet of tea?"

"No."

"Some buttermilk?"

"No."

"What, then? Yon's a nasty cough."

"Ay. Seems as I can't shift it since I come home."

"Then it's honey and allegar for you, my lad," said Esther, and she poured honey from a jar into a pan, added vinegar and warmed it on the fire, stirring the mixture. She tipped it into a mug and gave it to William.

"Get that down thee," she said.

"Ay!" William laughed. "That's about it! Honey and allegar. That reckons it up. It does. The whole beggaring cheese!" But he drank.

He went to the dresser. The shelves were laden with blue and white plates, their edges gilded, except for the one in the middle, the small one he had seen before.

He picked it up and looked at it closely.

"China. Eh, dear. Well, well."

He put it down.

"And all this effort? Have you grown a flavour for 'em, or what?"

"It was Yedart. At wedding."

"Yedart. Ay. He would. And gold and all. I did always say as he were a chap very fluent in giving."

William lifted the veil net and rolled it from her face.

"I'm back, Het."

"Ay."

"Same as I said."

"You did."

"What's that racket?"

The clapping sound could be heard from the other end of the house.

"William," said Esther. "He's at weaving silk: a little master. He works two markets. Stockport and Macclesfield. He weaves all hours."

"Is he mine?"

"He favours Yedart."

"But you called him Will?"

"I did."

"Ay."

"Leave him be, now."

"Yay."

He sat down again.

"What must we do, Het?"

"Do?"

"I'm back. Same as I said. I said I'd come. I told you. But you've not waited."

"Wait? Thirty odd year? You were transported, youth."

"But I said."

"Yay, and what was I to do? And Joseph's a good un. He took me and William, and never a word against him. 'No pobs without salt: no burying without laughing', Will."

"There's more nor pobs."

"It's all in your head, Will."

He sat for a long time, staring at the fire, silent.

"But I told you. Did you not hear?"

"I heard."

He stared again, for a longer time.

"What must I do, Het? I don't know what to do."

"Well, you can't just sit there, gondering. Shape yourself. You could go for a bricksetter."

"Eight month in chains I lay for thee."

"No."

"Me own water I supped for thee."

"Give over!"

"Eggy Mo I cut. For thee."

She gripped his wrist.

"And Eggy Mo I drank. For thee."

He was lost again in the fire.

"The Clashing Rock I dared. For thee."

"Eh?"

"The Hard Dark I walked. For thee. Bone of the Cloud I rode. For thee."

"Will, you make no sense."

"And could you not bide and wait for me?"

"But I never asked you. I never. It was you."

Silence again. Then he stood, and looked down at her.

"Was it? For nowt? Nowt then; and nowt now? All nowt?"

"Not nowt."

"Nowt. Me. Nowt. Back here. For this. Nowt. Nowt. Bugger Bunjil."

He slumped over the table, and Esther saw that there was no strength left to him, and that he was crying.

"Buck up, love," she said. " 'As long lives a merry man as a sorry.' "

"But where's me Dreaming?"

"Who's dreaming?"

"You'd best have this," he said, and he reached into his bag and took out the lifeless wallung and put it on the table. "I'm done. It's finished."

"The swaddledidaff!" said Esther. "You kept it!"

"Take it. You found it. It's yours. 'Tha conner hurt a brokken glass.' "

"No, Will," she said. "Our swaddledidaff. From me to thee."

She pushed it towards him, moved it into the sun. It caught the light and filled the room with colour.

" 'Pussy washing Dishes,' " said Esther to the patterns moving on the walls.

He watched, and felt a warmth and a memory return, and life in his face.

Thundal?

"Het."

Wallung.

"Het."

He lifted the crystal.

"Purranmurnin Tallarwurnin."

Thundal.

Oh, Het.

She smiled. "You daft ha'porth."

He put the thundal in his medicine bag. He unrolled the veil and covered her face and tucked the veil around her neck.

"I must be doing."

She went with him to the door.

"Be good, Will Buckley," said Esther.

"Be good, and then."

He strode away across the garden. The clap of the loom he now knew, and he danced for the man inside, whoever he was.

The dog whined, but stayed on the cop and did not follow.

Be good, Gyp.

He climbed Glaze Hill, shouted to the sky:

> "Kiminary keemo,
> Kiminary keemo,
> Kiminary, kiltikary, kiminary keemo!

String stram pammadilly, lamma pamma rat tag.
Ring dong bomminanny keemo!"

Before he left, he walked Esther's Dreaming. He walked the Holy
Well, by Saddlebole and Stormy Point to Golden Stone and Seven Firs
and Thieves' Hole, he walked the Beacon.

Then down from the ridge he walked for Buckley. He walked
Fernhill and Sodger's Hump. At Whisterfield he passed his Uncle
Jim's and looked in through the window of the room where he was
born. He walked Windy Harbour, Withington, Welltrough, over the
Tunstead and down to Gleads Moss and Trap Street, Clonter Brook,
and up to Mutlow. He walked, and sat beneath the trees on Mutlow.
He heard the songs of Neeyangarra in the wind among the stones.

And the hills around. A quietness settled on him. And in the quietness the Hamestan sang. He rose and went.

He felt a rhythm that began to fill him as he listened.

William Buckley left the Hamestan, to the oak. He entered in. He
reached for the jackstones down the hollow. He took out the shiny
pebbles. And now he saw they were not jackstones, but blades of flint.
The People had made them: Yambeetch and Warrowil. The People
had known the oak. One tree was all, and all the world one Dreaming.

He looked up. Cush, cush. Cush-a-cush.

He put the flints in the medicine bag, and dug with his hands in
the leaf mould until he came to the charcoal of the fire. He took the
charcoal and rubbed it into his face. Then he tore two branches from
the living wood, and Shick-Shack went down from the oak and into
the bowl that had been the mere. He kicked off his shoes and felt the
land. He stood, holding the branches upright. The mere was waiting.
Under the ground he felt the water run.

" – For fear you make the golden bird to weep."

He put a green branch around each shoulder, his black face, and
went to the church, and in by the belfry.

nephew and for the warriors. His feet woke slowly, but he did not stop; and he heard the rug drums and the clapsticks, and the People were singing. He danced faster, and they lifted him and the choir was filled with them.

Then he danced the Morning Star, and left the altar, dancing, and the hollow logs beneath the chancel and the nave boomed as he stamped. He danced the Morning Star. The windows flared hollin, coraminga, cuckoo bread; torumba, nardoo, galligaskins; devilberry, jackanapes, goborro, mulkathandra; vervey, bolwarra, popple, marara; karagata, dargan, Robin-run-in-th'hedge. And the East sent a rainbow to the mere of the font. He danced in the rainbow and about the trees, in the drums and the song, and he danced at the font for the Man in the Oak and the Crown of Glory, but the eyes were blind.

He left the drumming and the song and danced into Silence. The paint and the bright sweat melted to air.

Through the Silence came the voice of Tundun, and he danced, beyond mulla-mullung, he danced the Evening Star. His step was with the voice of Tundun. He danced the Evening Star to bring the warriors home, and made the path of Murrangurk's five ways. He danced the Evening Star for the blind eyes in the crown; and the eyes of the glass opened, and Nullamboin looked at him.

The church was light and the scent of oak and the scent of bwal. From the South door lay the bush of Beangala to the sea. Tundun and the Silence and the Song were All and One.

Strandloper entered into his bone country. The wave bore his right foot, and the earth his left. He walked with Binbeal, son of Bunjil.

There came an eagle.

Here is the start of the Dream,
and how the sweet sorrow is sung.

The framing of the tower enclosed him as the oak, and split light, dappled swaddledidaff, through the glass. And one small piece of red, round glass was Neeyangarra rising on his wings of flame.

Shick-Shack entered the nave, and smelt the forest of the church.

Before him, the East Window was filled with churingas and Dreamings, and the coiling length of Binbeal and the interweaving circles of the Three Points of Time. In the biggest churinga was a man in red and white, speaking Wurunjerri-baluk with his fingers and saying: All.

He stood at the dry stone font and gripped the rim of two of the sides. Across were the South door and the window of the Man in the Oak and the Crown of Glory. He looked into the blind eyes of the sleeping god, and saw the face of his nephew, painted in the way of his first Dreaming, above the solemn path of the snake, black on a white headband, its fires marked with a dot in the curve of each bend, and his churinga below.

> "Water of life, water of death,
> Each has my soul fed.
> Sun, river and thunder
> Give me new breath."

He held the crystal in the font, and the mere bubbled up the stone to the rim. He scooped his hand to drink.

He lifted the branches against a pillar. He put the medicine bag on the font and took out balls of clay: white, black, yellow and red. He pulled off his clothes, and, slowly, he painted his body with the clay, using the font to work a paste.

Murrangurk painted his own Dreamings and his People. He tied on his headband and set kowir and plover in his hair, and the feather from an eagle's wing. He put koim through his nose. And when he had finished, he went and laid the branches on the altar, and turned to face the church.

Mulla-mullung moved him, and he danced the Crow, for his